THE THREAD OF EVIDENCE

A Sixties Mystery

BERNARD KNIGHT

D1379493

First published in Great Britain by Robert Hale Ltd 1965
This edition published by Accent Press 2015

ISBN 9781910939994

Author's Note

The Sixties Mysteries is a series of reissues of my early crime stories, the first of which was originally published in 1963. Looking back now, it is evident how criminal investigation has changed over the last half-century. Though basic police procedure is broadly the same, in these pages you will find no Crime Scene Managers or Crown Prosecution Service, no DNA, CSI, PACE, nor any of the other acronyms beloved of modern novels and television. These were the days when detectives still wore belted raincoats and trilby hats. There was no Health and Safety to plague us and the police smoked and drank tea alongside the post-mortem table!

Modern juries are now more interested in the reports of the forensic laboratory than in the diligent labours of the humble detective, though it is still the latter that solves most serious crimes. This is not to by any means belittle the enormous advances made in forensic science in recent years, but to serve as a reminder that the old murder teams did a pretty good job based simply on experience and dogged investigation.

Bernard Knight
2015

Original Author's Note

Neither the Cardiganshire Constabulary nor a Chair in Forensic Medicine at Swansea exist, in fact. Apologies are due to both the Home Office and the University of Wales for the arbitrary rearrangement of their departments!

Chapter One

The taller of the two men raised his cap to the young lady who opened the door.

'I'm sorry to disturb you on a Sunday afternoon, miss, but I wondered if the doctor was at home.'

He jerked his head at a bundle wrapped in newspaper, which his companion held reverently in his hands.

'You see, we think we may have found a bit of a body!'

Mary Ellis-Morgan stared blankly at them for a few seconds. As the daughter and housekeeper of the local doctor, she thought she had seen every kind of medical emergency, but to be faced by two slightly embarrassed men clutching what they alleged to be part of a corpse, was something outside even her experience.

'Er … yes – yes, he is in. I'll call him for you.'

Her wits rapidly returned and she opened the door wider. 'You'd better come in and wait in the surgery – it's through here.'

Mary ushered them into the hall and through another door into a waiting room furnished with a collection of odd chairs, an electric fire and a pile of tattered magazines.

'I'll call him from the garden. He won't be a moment.'

She closed the door and hurried back to the kitchen at the rear of the house. Opening the window, she called out to her father, who was sitting on the lawn in a deckchair, talking to a younger man.

'Daddy, there's someone in the surgery to see you.'

'Very well – I'm coming.'

Without enthusiasm, the doctor hoisted himself from his chair and walked slowly towards the surgery annexe at the far end of the house.

Pausing only long enough to give a tidying pat to her red hair, Mary passed through the kitchen door and crossed the lawn to where her fiancé sprawled drowsily in his deckchair. As she plumped down alongside him, Peter Adams shaded his eyes against the September sun and peered at her quizzically.

'What's going on?' he demanded.

'Nothing much,' she replied with studied casualness. 'Just a couple of men with a parcel for Daddy. They said they had found some human remains.'

'Huh-huh!'

The sun was warm and Peter lay back in his chair, eyes closed again, his brain hardly registering. Mary sat watching him, smiling affectionately and patiently waiting for her words to arouse the journalist's instinct within him that was never very far below the surface. The penny dropped and Peter sat up abruptly.

'What did you say?' he asked, blinking owlishly at her.

'Two men called about some human remains,' she repeated, her eyes glinting with mischief.

'What sort of human remains?'

'I couldn't see. They were wrapped in newspaper.'

'Wrapped in newspaper! Good God, do you mean that these two characters brought the stuff in handfuls?'

She nodded. 'For Daddy's opinion. I'm glad I'm not in his place, aren't you? Fancy having to unwrap that stuff!'

'But these two men,' he persisted, not to be sidetracked, 'where did they find these relics?'

'I don't know, darling.'

'Well, for goodness' sake, didn't you ask them?'

'I did not! I've been a receptionist to three busy GPs for long enough to have learnt some of the tricks of the trade! And the first is never to ask questions if you don't want to be swamped by the symptoms of every patient who comes to the house.'

2

'But these men weren't patients,' he objected in exasperation. 'This is incredible. Two men knock on your door, announcing the find of the century, and all you can think of doing is to ask them to step into the surgery!'

'That's right, darling,' she admitted sweetly. 'But, then, I'm not a newshound like you. I don't think of every titbit of news in terms of flaming headlines.'

Peter rolled his eyes skywards in supplication.

'And to think that I shall soon be joined in holy wedlock with this woman who describes as "titbits of news" whole corpses wrapped in newspaper!' He began to climb to his feet. 'Excuse me, my sweet, but this is an act I really must get in on.'

'You needn't bother to get up,' Mary told him, looking across her shoulder towards the house. 'You're too late. Here comes Daddy now. I expect he'll tell you as much as he thinks is good for you.'

Peter turned his head and saw the doctor coming across the lawn towards them.

Slight of build, with kindly twinkling eyes, his sparse hair plastered back over his head to give the maximum coverage, he looked ten years younger than his sixty-four years. As Peter watched, it occurred to him that he had never seen this man dressed in anything other than the baggy grey tweed suit that he was now wearing; *probably*, he thought, *he'll turn up in it at church next year to give his only daughter away in marriage.*

Pulling up another chair for the older man as he joined them, Peter asked, 'What was all that about? Mary has been hinting at something horrific!'

'Well, so it was, in a way,' the doctor replied in his staccato North Walian accent. 'It could turn out to be quite nasty, I suppose. The two chaps who have just left are on holiday from Coventry, here in the village. This afternoon, it seems, their kids come galloping home from a jaunt on the cliffs brandishing a human femur. One of the men thought he recognized it for what it was and brought it to me for confirmation.'

'A human femur! That's the thigh bone, isn't it? Where the devil did they find it?'

'Picked it up in a cave, they said, but it's more likely to have been an old mine working. The cliffs are riddled with them. There's no doubt about the bone being human, though.'

'There, Peter darling,' Mary said consolingly, 'you've got your precious headlines at last: – "How I found the missing link!".'

Peter grinned at her. 'The *Morning News* doesn't go much on archaeology, I'm afraid. But it might be worth a try.'

'You can forget about archaeology,' the doctor interrupted. 'The bone's old, but not all that old.'

'How old, then?' Peter asked with quickening interest.

'Twenty – fifty – a hundred, perhaps. I'm no expert in such things, but it's certainly not a museum piece.'

'Then it's a police job, eh? Have you told Wynne Griffith?'

'I've just phoned his house, but he was out. His wife promised to get him to ring back as soon as he comes in.'

'How much of a body do you have to find before it becomes of interest to the law, I wonder?' Mary asked thoughtfully.

Her father shrugged his shoulders. 'Don't ask me,' he said. 'Forensic medicine is way off my beat as a country GP – I've forgotten all I ever mugged up for the exam as a student. Presumably, the bit must be big enough, or vital enough, to suggest that death has occurred. I don't suppose a little finger on its own would interest a coroner, but a thigh bone could only come either from an operating theatre or a corpse.'

Mary thought of her two brothers, the other members of the medical practice that the Ellis-Morgans ran in this quiet seaside village on the west coast of Wales.

'A pity that Gerry and David aren't here this evening,' she said. 'Gerry is supposed to be the local police surgeon – and, the only time that anything has *ever* happened, he's down in Swansea on a cricket weekend.'

'They'd have liked to have been in on it, no doubt,' agreed their father. 'But the police are sure to get their own forensic expert up to look at it before very long.'

They sat discussing the discovery while the autumn sun slid down the sky towards the west.

Mary lay back most of the time, listening to the men. She saw that her fiancé was getting more and more fidgety as the time went by.

'Oh, Peter, for goodness' sake, stop looking at your watch!' she scolded. 'PC Griffith isn't going to get home any quicker for you twitching with impatience!'

Peter forced his tall body back into his chair in an effort to look relaxed.

The doctor's eyes twinkled behind his big horn-rimmed glasses.

'There you are, my boy; you're being nagged already. You'd better give up working for that newspaper in Cardiff – she won't let you go out late at night when you're married!'

Peter grinned sheepishly. 'I'm supposed to be on holiday and *this* breaks on the second day. I don't know if it's good or bad luck.'

John Ellis-Morgan tapped his pipe bowl on the chair frame with quick nervous movements. Peter thought again how bird-like he was, his sudden jerky movements and his pattering walk being like those of a lively little sparrow.

'May be nothing much in it, Peter,' warned the doctor. 'So don't get your notebook out yet – though I can't imagine how a femur could get into an old lead mine without some funny business being involved somewhere.'

Peter rose to his feet restlessly and stood with his hands

in his pockets, staring up at the green cliff which almost overhung the house above the surgery.

'These mines are up there somewhere, are they?' he asked.

Mary's father jabbed the air with the stem of his pipe. 'Yes, but a fair way along the top from here – there are more on that side, too.'

He waved towards the opposite side of the large garden, where an almost identical fern-covered hill reared up into the evening sky.

Carmel House, the Ellis-Morgans' home, was built in the narrow valley where a stream cut its way through the rampart of cliffs that formed the coastline of Cardigan Bay. The village of Tremabon lay a quarter of a mile further inland, abreast the main road that ran from Aberystwyth to Cardigan. The steep green slopes that Peter Adams was so impatiently studying were the landward buttresses of the plateau that fell almost sheer into the sea on the other side.

Mary leant forwards and jabbed a sharp finger into her fiancé's ribs.

'If there's any reporting to be done, you can count yourself out, my lad – you're mine for a fortnight, remember? The *South Wales Morning News* can go to pot until then.'

Any retort that Peter may have intended was frozen by the sound of the telephone ringing in the house. The doctor hopped up and began pattering across the smooth grass.

'That will be Griffith now, I expect,' he said unnecessarily over his shoulder.

Peter hesitated, then began to follow. A firm tug on the back of his sports coat brought him up short.

'Oh, no you don't! You sit down and be nice to me. If I'm no match for a dirty old bone, you'd better have your ring back!'

The determination beneath her flippant words was

plain, and Peter flopped back into his chair with a sigh.

'All right, Ginger, you win.'

'I'm not *ginger* – it's auburn,' pouted his girlfriend. 'But seriously, pet, do you think this bone business could be important – I mean, you know, criminal or anything?'

'Bones only get buried in queer places when the death has been unusual,' replied Peter. 'If it turns out only to be the one bone there, then there may be some innocent explanation.'

'What do you mean?'

'I remember a devil of a fuss when I was in college because a medical student left an ear from the dissecting room on the top floor of a bus. And the fellow I shared my digs with always had bits of his skeleton scattered about the house. But, apart from that sort of thing, I can't see how a thigh bone could turn up in a lead mine unless someone had deliberately hidden it there.'

Mary still looked doubtful.

'But there are some ancient barrows on the cliffs, too. Couldn't this be some sort of old ritual burial?'

Peter shook his head. 'Not in a lead mine, sweet. I don't know much about them, but I think the oldest only go back to Roman times.'

'Perhaps it was a mining accident,' Mary said hopefully.

Peter smiled affectionately at her.

'You're determined to do my paper out of a sensation, aren't you? Your father said that he thought the thing wasn't all that old – so it's no good you trying to push this business back to the dawn of time.'

On the telephone, John Ellis-Morgan was having trouble of the opposite kind, trying to repress the local constable's enthusiasm from getting out of hand.

'Now, now, Wynne, go easy until we've found out a bit more about it,' he soothed in Welsh. Griffith had already excitedly offered to call in everyone, including Scotland

Yard and Interpol.

'You come over here now and we'll go up to the cliff with these children,' he went on. 'There may be something else up there, if they're not pulling our leg – though I can't see where they'd get a femur from.'

Griffith hurriedly agreed and the doctor hung up.

Over in the police house on the other side of the village, the constable slammed the telephone down and darted back into the living room, where his wife and small son were having tea.

'Pass me my jacket, love, quick,' he said with feverish haste. 'I've got to get over to Dr John's right away!'

His wife looked at him calmly.

'What's all the rush, Wynne – have the Russians landed on Tremabon beach or something?'

His son gazed at his father as the policeman struggled with his blue coat. Griffith was normally a calm, stolid man; and this sudden activity was unusual enough to make the five-year-old stare at him wide-eyed, a spoonful of jelly poised before his mouth.

'Well, what's it all about, I said?' repeated his wife sharply.

'Some boys have found a human bone up on the south cliff and taken it to the doctor. I'm off now to see what it's all about – might be the biggest thing I've ever had!'

He dived into the tiny hall and pushed his large upright bicycle through the front door. His wife watched impassively. Motoring offences, hayrick fires and human bones were all one to her.

Griffith leapt onto his machine and rode off down the hill into Tremabon. The white house with the blue 'Police' sign over the door was on the outskirts of the village on the road north to Aberystwyth. To reach Carmel House, he had to go down to the crossroads in the centre of the hamlet and turn off into the lane that led down to the beach through the gap in the cliffs.

A man in his middle thirties, he was a good officer, steady and reliable. Like many country policemen, he was professionally frustrated. The most heinous crimes that normally came his way were the absence of lights on pedal cycles and the failure of farmers to dip their sheep at the specified times. Rare events like the theft of the vicar's rose bushes or the fatal collapse of Mrs Hughes at the bus stop were milestones in his career. The present prospect of a human bone on his ground was the greatest event since he'd had his helmet. *At least it means an inquest*, he thought, *and* – dare he hope? – *the possibility of criminal proceedings*.

While the constable was furiously pedalling through the lanes in a turmoil of anticipation, John Ellis-Morgan had telephoned the guest house nearby and asked the fathers to bring their small sons across.

By the time PC Griffith arrived, a little group had formed on the wide gravel drive of Carmel House, ready to meet him.

Griffith managed to suppress his excitement under a gruff official manner. After being introduced to the holidaymakers, he turned back to the garden gates.

'Right, we'll get on up there, then.'

Peter, in defiance of Mary's threats, was determined not to miss anything. He knew the constable quite well, both from shooting trips and meetings in the local public house.

'Mind if I come up, Wynne? This sounds interesting.'

Griffith nodded, but there was a cautious look on his face.

'I suppose it's all right, Mr Adams – but you won't go writing anything in your paper, will you? At least, not until you have a word with my inspector.'

Peter laughed off the other's fears.

'I'm on holiday, Wynne – so don't worry.'

Given this ambiguous assurance, the constable set off up the cliff path opposite the gates of the house. With Peter bringing up the rear, the little party followed a winding sheep track through the bracken. Climbing higher and higher up the steep slope, they saw the house shrink in size until it looked like a toy below them. The village behind them came into sight, resembling a medieval map spread out at the top of the valley.

The little doctor began to puff with exertion, and even the constable had to remove his helmet to mop the sweat from his brow. The sun was on the horizon, but it was still warm as they finally reached the summit of the cliff and found themselves on the fairly level grass at the top.

They paused for a breather and Peter looked seawards at the great sweep of Cardigan Bay which was now visible.

'My God, what a view!' exclaimed one of the Coventry visitors, taking in the wall of cliffs marching to the horizon on either side, with the green sea and white rollers at their feet.

The policeman was in no mood for scenery and started off along the ridge to the south. On their right, the smooth grass and ferns swept down to the limestone crags which fell sheer into the breakers.

'Along here, was it, sonny?' Griffith asked one of the little boys. He was the elder of the two, a carrotty-haired child of about seven.

'Yes, a bit farther on. I'll show you,' chirped the boy. He pranced ahead, the other one racing after him, afraid to be left out of the limelight.

They stopped at the edge of a little ravine and waited for the grown-ups to come.

The first lad pointed across at the other side of the little valley.

'There it is, sir. That hole in the ground.'

Peter and Wynne looked blankly at the other side.

'I can't see anything. Can you?' asked the doctor.

All that was visible on the further bank were some gorse bushes and a few stony outcrops.

'I'll show you,' yelled the red-haired boy and charged down into the gully, his legs going like pistons to keep up with his headlong flight. A scraggy sheep stampeded blindly from his path and some gulls rose, screaming abuse into the blue sky.

'Here it is, Dad!' yelled the boy. He appeared to be pointing at an outcrop of grey stone; but, as the adults moved nearer, Peter could see that a patch of ferns and stunted gorse hid the opening of a shaft, which faced out to sea.

A crude ramp, overgrown and crumbling, led to the mouth and the men climbed up to join the two boys.

'It was in here, Dad,' said the elder.

'I found it first, honest,' yelled the little one, determined not to be outdone.

John Ellis-Morgan peered into the dark hole.

'It's a lead mine all right, not a natural cave. I've been in a few of them up here in my younger days; but I never remember seeing this one before.'

'I'm not surprised,' commented Peter. 'The opening faces the cliff. So, unless you happen to be a seagull, you would be hardly likely to notice it.'

The PC was pulling a large torch from his pocket.

'New batteries, this week,' he explained needlessly.

Removing his helmet, he plunged into the entrance. Immediately there was a muffled curse in Welsh and he backed out, rubbing his forehead.

'Piece of rock hanging down just inside,' he muttered to the doctor. 'Better stay here until I see what it's like. The roof seems half-collapsed.'

He put his helmet on again and went back inside, bending low to get his six foot two frame into the passage.

The others waited expectantly around the mouth of the mine.

'This place can't have been used for donkey's years, surely?' asked one of the holidaymakers.

Ellis-Morgan shrugged, his shoulders twitching in his characteristic sparrow fashion. 'Certainly not in my time, and I've been here thirty years. I think some of them were worked up until the First World War; but not on this part of the cliffs. It may well have been generations since they took ore from this place.'

Peter was standing at the opening, watching the constable's wavering light go deeper into the heart of the cliff.

'How far in did you find the bone, sonny?' he asked the ginger boy, who was crouched at his feet.

'About twice the length of a house,' the lad replied graphically. 'We couldn't go any further – there was a big heap of stones and our candles were getting dim.'

Peter grinned at the boy's father. 'Boys never change, do they?'

There was an echoing call from the bowels of the earth. 'Dr John – can you come in now?'

Griffith was shouting from the deepest point he could reach and the words had an eerie sound by the time they got to the shaft entrance.

Ellis-Morgan dragged a torch from his own pocket and shouted a reply:

'Right, Wynne. I'm coming now.'

Leaving the other men clustered around the entrance, he vanished into the shaft. Being many inches shorter than the policeman, he was able to walk upright once inside the tunnel. The floor was cluttered with pieces of fallen rock but, apart from pools of muddy water, he found the going fairly easy.

Griffith's torch wavered ahead of him, growing larger as he approached.

He came up to the officer at a point which he roughly estimated as being thirty yards from the entrance.

'The roof's come down here, Doctor.'

The constable spoke in Welsh now that they were away from the holidaymakers.

The doctor shone his torch over the end of the shaft. An avalanche of grey stone had completely blocked the tunnel, leaving a great abyss in the roof over their heads.

'A fairly recent fall, Wynne. This stone is cleaner and a lighter colour than the walls.'

Griffith waggled the spotlight of his torch on to the ground at their feet.

'And look here, Dr John – what's this?'

Ellis-Morgan hitched up his trousers and squatted at the edge of the roof fall. An inch of murky water covered the floor, but a muddy brown object could still be seen sticking out from beneath a stone.

'Give me a hand to move some of this rock,' commanded the doctor. They began pulling away the stones at the bottom of the heap.

Ellis-Morgan uncovered the whole of the brown stick-like thing and held it up to the beam of his torch.

'This is another bone, boy,' he chirped. 'No doubt about it being human; it's a forearm bone.'

The PC was almost beside himself with excitement.

'Duw, Doctor. The whole skeleton may be just under these stones here.'

He began scrabbling furiously at the bottom of the pile, pulling out stones of all sizes and dropping them into the muddy water, oblivious of the damage to his uniform trousers.

'Here's some more – and a couple there!'

The physician began fishing out more fragments as Griffith uncovered them.

'There's another big one,' said the excited constable, as he lifted a particularly large rock.

The doctor had barely grabbed it when there was an ominous rumble and an avalanche of stone slid down to fill in their excavation completely.

Ellis-Morgan hastily backed away.

'Better leave it for now. Otherwise we'll have the whole lot down on top of us.'

He picked up the bundle of remains and turned to the entrance.

'Let's go and see what we've already found looks like in the open.'

They made their way back to the impatient group at the mouth of the shaft, to emerge, mud-spattered and blinking, into the evening light.

Peter pounced on his father-in-law-to-be. 'What did you find in there? Are those more bones?'

'Hold on, lad. Let's put these down somewhere.' The doctor spread his finds on the grassy bank at the side of the old ramp.

'Now then, let's see how much anatomy I remember after forty-odd years.'

He studied the grubby collection as the others clustered around to look over his shoulders.

'This is a radius – from the forearm. And these two are ribs,' he said, holding them up.

'And this is a vertebra – from the spine. And this.'

He laid some more ribs out in a neat row.

'What's that big one?' asked the ever-impatient Peter.

'Ah, that's the prize of the collection, Griffith – the one we found last.' He picked it up. It was a bone about a foot long, with knobs at either end.

'This is the bone from the upper arm – the humerus. And this is a right-sided one,' the doctor proudly explained.

'They don't look much like the bones my student pal used to have,' objected Peter. 'They were smooth and white.'

'And they hadn't been lying in mud and water for umpteen years, either,' countered Ellis-Morgan. 'These

14

have got half an inch of mud stuck to them.'

He rubbed the arm bone vigorously in the grass to clean it.

'That's better – what's this, I wonder?'

The doctor jerked his glasses back up his nose with a finger, and peered short-sightedly at the bone.

He picked at something with a fingernail while the others waited expectantly.

After a long moment, he squinted at the constable over the top of his spectacles.

'Wynne, perhaps you'll get those sergeant's stripes out of this after all!'

He tapped the bone as he spoke.

'There's a saw cut here. Just below the shoulder!'

Chapter Two

'I always said that it was him that had done it!'

The speaker gave a final rub to the pint glass and hung it on its hook over the bar.

His audience on the other side of the counter, nodded in unison. Three tankards were lifted to their lips as if to put a seal of approval on the landlord's judgement.

'How did you come to know of it so soon, Ceri?' asked one of the men, a wizened old fellow in a crumpled felt hat. Ceri Lloyd, the landlord of the Lamb and Flag, Tremabon's only public house, leant his enormous body across the small bar in a gesture of confidence.

'Lewis John the Post Office came in about an hour ago,' he hissed in a loud stage whisper. 'His missus was on the switchboard when Wynne Griffith put a call through from the doctor's house to his inspector in Aber – heard it all, she did.'

''T isn't right, that,' one of the other men muttered into his beer. 'That nosy old bitch will cause some trouble one of these days.'

He was recollecting some rather indiscreet telephone calls which he had recently made himself.

'Well, she did, anyhow,' carried on Lloyd – his cascade of chins wobbling as he strove to impart his confidential news to the whole of the crowded bar parlour. 'Griffith was reporting some bones that him and Dr John had just found.'

'You've told us all that once already,' complained the third man, a ruddy-faced old boy with 'farmer' written all over him. 'What I want to know is, why you think it's anything to do with Roland Hewitt's missus?'

'Well, stands to reason, don't it?' said Ceri. He moved away for a moment to draw a pint for another customer. The small low room held a dozen or more regulars, and they sat with their ears almost flapping to catch the scandal that was being dispensed from the bar as freely as the ale.

Ceri rang the price of the pint into his till and draped himself back over the pumps.

'Stands to reason, I said – how many other women have we ever had vanish from Tremabon, eh, Jenkin?' His piggy eyes challenged the man with the battered hat.

'How do you know this here body is a woman, anyway?' Jenkin had come in later than the others and was a step behind in the gossip.

'The doctor told Griffith. That's all he could say about it, according to Lewis John's wife – that and the fact that the body had been cut up into little pieces.'

The constable's mention of one saw cut had already been magnified into utter dismemberment by the villagers. The landlord slapped a podgy hand on the counter.

'So there, Jenkin – I ask you again, what woman has gone from Tremabon in suspicious circumstances, eh?'

There was dead silence in the bar. All heads were turned to look at the great fat publican.

He savoured the moment, his drooping lips rolling a cigarette butt around, before delivering the denouement.

'Mavis Hewitt, of course – you know that as well as I do.'

Crumpled-hat nodded grudgingly. 'Ay, it was a rare old fuss at the time. But, damn it, that was more than thirty year ago – a hell of a long while back!'

'And these here bones go a long way back, too, by the sound of it,' Ceri hissed triumphantly.

A young man wearing a bus driver's uniform moved up from the end of the bar.

'What's all the mystery about old Hewitt, Ceri?' he

asked. 'You old jossers seem to know something pretty salty about him.'

Ceri looked down from his six foot frame of gross obesity. 'You're too much of a kid to remember, boy. But your dad would know about it.'

'Remember what?'

'You know Roland Hewitt, you say?'

'Yes, everybody does. He lives in that blue cottage up off the Cardigan road. Came from Canada a few years back to retire here. It's his nephew that's courting the doctor's daughter.'

The publican nodded condescendingly. 'You've got it – but did you know that he was born in Tremabon and lived here at Bryn Glas farm until nineteen twenty-nine? Then he skipped out of the country, he did. Just after his wife vanished, it was.'

The young man stared at Lloyd over his glass. 'What d'you mean – skipped the country?'

Jenkin of the crumpled trilby hat took up the story. 'Things were getting too hot for him – I remember it like it was yesterday. The papers had a hold of it, and the police were nosing about Bryn Glas. So Hewitt packed up and cleared off to Canada. Mighty quick, he was, too.'

'Well, what did happen to his wife, anyway?' asked the bus driver, looking back to Ceri Lloyd.

The landlord took up another glass to polish.

'Nobody knows – or didn't until today,' he leered. 'She just vanished. Her sister came down from Liverpool and started the ball rolling. Raised a devil of fuss, she did; but nothing came of it. Old Hewitt was too clever for all of them.'

The young man looked scornful.

'I think you're all a lot of bloody old women making a scandal out of damn all!'

The publican was outraged at the bus driver's impudent challenge to his leadership of the gossip.

19

'And what d'you think you know about it, Gareth Hughes? You were still a twinkle in your old man's eye then. Listen, I knew Mavis Hewitt better than most around here. I know what went on up at Bryn Glas all right!'

Jenkin's leathery face wrinkled as he sniggered evilly. 'You knew her all right, Ceri – *you* were half the cause of the trouble between her and old Roland, I reckon.'

Far from being offended, the fat landlord actually preened himself.

'Well, I'm not denying that I had a way with the girls when I was a bit younger – before I grew this.' He patted his great stomach affectionately.

The bus driver gulped his beer impatiently and slapped it down for a refill. 'You still haven't said what the connection is between this bone business and old Hewitt.'

'Are you daft, man?' demanded Ceri, as he drew another pint. 'Roland did his wife in, back in twenty-nine – hid the body up on the cliff and hopped it abroad. Plain as the nose on your face, it is!'

Gareth Hughes made a rude noise. 'Get away, man! What would he want to come back here for, after all those years?'

Ceri gazed at him pityingly. 'Haven't you ever heard that murderers always come back to the scene of their crime – always?'

The bus driver sneered. 'You old geezers love making mountains out of molehills, don't you? If I were you, I'd watch what you say. Hewitt could have the law on you for slander. And, if the police knew that that old crow in the post office was listening to their secrets, they'd lock her up.' He poured the rest of his beer straight down his throat and walked out of the bar.

The red-faced farmer glared after him indignantly. 'Think they know it all, these young chaps. I remember Mavis Hewitt well enough myself – pretty little thing, she was. Red hair and a lovely pair of ankles on her.' Long-forgotten lust shone in his bleary eyes for a brief moment. Ceri licked his fleshy lips at memories of his own.

'The only lively bit of goods we ever had in this damn village. The women used to hate her, just because she used to turn all their husbands' heads in the road.' He paused and slowly rolled his eternal cigarette butt from one corner of his mouth to the other.

'Yes, quite a piece, was Mavis – younger than old Hewitt by a good few years. Only been married about eighteen months when she disappeared.'

'How old do you reckon she'd be then?' asked the farmer.

Ceri scratched the stubble on his vast chin.

'Let's see. She was two years younger than me – that would make her born in nineteen oh-three, so she'd be twenty-six.'

Leather-face came back into the conversation. 'In gentleman's service, she was, as far as I remember.'

'Yes, a parlourmaid until Hewitt got hold of her. English girl originally, from Liverpool.'

The red-cheeked farmer contemplated the froth on his bitter.

'As far as I recall it, Hewitt said that she had walked out on him after a row. I never did see why there was all that fuss and commotion. Nothing so unusual in a wife leaving her old man, is there?'

Lloyd answered with the assurance of one with inside information.

'That's not the half of it – and them fights they had, well, the poor girl was left black and blue. She showed me some of the bruises herself,' he added archly.

Battered Hat leered at him over the pumps.

'I'll bet she did! I know you were pretty thick with her, Ceri – even *after* they were married, eh?'

The landlord winked lewdly at him.

'Aye, quite a girl was Mavis. Damn, I was upset when

she vanished. I missed my little bit of fun of an afternoon. I was that mad, I accused Roland to his face. He's never spoken to me from that day to this. Hates my guts, I reckon.'

Jenkin nodded agreement.

'Queer chap. Keeps himself to himself. Civil enough to me, I'll admit. But there's something odd about him. Too fond of the chapel, I say. They're always a bit odd, them very religious types.'

'He's got enough cause to be queer, with *that* on his conscience,' Ceri said stubbornly. 'Probably goes to chapel to try to wash out his sins.'

'That nephew of his – the one on the paper in Cardiff – he seems a nice enough young chap,' observed the farmer.

'Yes, he's a nice bloke – comes in here quite often for a drink. He stays with the old man quite a lot since he's taken up with Mary Ellis-Morgan.'

The wrinkled old man at once became animated.

'Now *there's* a grand girl for you – that Miss Ellis-Morgan. Always got a smile when you go down to the surgery. Nothing's too much trouble for her. I don't know how those three doctors down at Carmel would get on without her.'

Ceri agreed. 'Two bachelors and a widower like her father must take a bit of looking after. About time those two boys found themselves a wife.'

'Some hope of that in Tremabon. All the young people clear off as soon as they can. It's a wonder that David and Gerald haven't moved to some more lively place.'

Ceri frowned at the dialogue between his two customers, which was stealing his thunder over the news of the bones.

'I wonder what doctor the police will get, to look at these remains,' he said, pointedly bringing the conversation back onto his own tack.

'What's going to happen next, then?' asked Jenkin.

Jenkin made a disbelieving noise in the back of his throat. 'All right! All right! But it was you that started it, Ceri Lloyd,' he countered. 'It was your idea that this might be Mavis's body, don't forget. You seem mighty anxious to get all the blame fair and square on old Hewitt's shoulders. Are you afraid the police are going to nab *you* for it? You were mighty thick with her, weren't you? The bobbies will be glad of a chat with you, I expect.'

While this fine wrangle was building up in the bar parlour of the inn, Peter was driving through the semi-dusk to his uncle's cottage. He'd stayed with Roland Hewitt, his mother's brother, quite often since he had become first friendly, and then engaged, to Mary Ellis-Morgan. He had first come to Tremabon about three years before, to see his uncle for the first time since he came back to Wales from Canada. On that very first visit, he had met Mary; and, ever since, he had travelled the ninety miles from Cardiff almost every couple of weeks for all-too-brief weekend trips. The longer summer holiday, like the present one, was something to look forward to all the year. He suddenly realized, as he drove through the quiet lanes, that this would be the last. Before next autumn, they would be married and living in a Cardiff suburb.

Peter turned his Morris off the main road to Cardigan, about half a mile south of the village, and drove up a lonely track lined by tall hedgerows. His uncle lived in an isolated cottage with a couple of acres of land. He kept poultry and a few pigs there, more for something to occupy his time than for profit.

The macadamized lane soon petered out to become a rough track for the last few hundred yards. In spite of this unpromising approach, the cottage was neat and well-kept.

Backed by a clump of wind-stunted trees, the low building nestled in a slight hollow. The cottage had been a farm in the old days and a barn built up against one side served as a garage for Peter's car.

He drove in through the open doors and stopped the engine. A furious barking inside the house told him that Twm, his uncle's sheepdog, had heard him arrive. By the time he had locked up the barn, his uncle was on the doorstep to meet him, the dog thumping his tail in welcome at Roland's feet.

'You're late, boy. I thought you were coming home early to take a gun out on the cliffs?'

Peter patted the dog as they went into the cottage.

'We've had a bit of excitement down at Carmel House, so I forgot all about Twm and his rabbits, I'm afraid. Then I called in the Lamb for a minute, but I think they'd all gone soft in the head there tonight!'

His uncle frowned as they entered the stone-flagged kitchen.

'I don't know why you go there, boy. I don't say anything about you having a drink – in moderation, of course. But that creature Lloyd, ugh! He's a bad lot, if ever there was.'

Peter had gathered on several occasions that there was no love lost between his uncle and the publican of the Lamb and Flag, but he had never been able to get the old man to talk about it.

'What was all this excitement you were just talking about?' Roland sat in his big wheel-back chair at the fireside and peered benignly at his nephew through his old-fashioned steel-rimmed spectacles, with their thick pebble lenses. He was a small man, whose frail appearance hid a wiry body. Though sixty-nine years of age, he ran his smallholding without any outside help.

Peter settled himself in a more modern chair on the other side of the huge black-leaded cooking range.

'Some young kids found a human bone up on the south cliff,' he began to explain. 'They brought it to Dr John. Later on we went up with Griffith, the policeman, to have a look.'

Roland leant forward with interest, his pale blue eyes flickering behind his glasses.

'Where was this, then?'

'In an old mine shaft – one of the levels that they used to work for lead. When we went back, sure enough, there were a lot more bones there – probably from a young woman.'

'Well, well! Were they very old, these bones?'

Peter shook his head.

'Mary's father doesn't think so – but we won't know until the experts come up tomorrow. The most interesting thing is that one of the arm bones has a saw cut halfway through it.'

Roland looked blankly at his nephew. 'What does that mean?'

'Someone must have been messing about with the body after death. And, of course, the fact that the body was so well hidden is highly suspicious in itself.'

Roland was silent. He stared into the fire for a long moment.

'The police are coming tomorrow, you say?'

Peter nodded, sensing a change in the old man's mood. *What the devil's wrong in Tremabon?* he wondered, the bar parlour fresh in his mind. As soon as the bones were mentioned, people started to act oddly.

Roland spoke again, still gazing into the embers of the grate.

'So they must think there's some foul play involved here?'

Peter nodded again. 'Seems a strong possibility.'

'That means murder, does it, boy?'

Roland's voice was decidedly strange now, thought Peter.

'I suppose so. The saw cut is the thing that matters.' He spoke quite cheerfully, but watched his uncle carefully this time. He was certain that something unusual was going on in the old chap's mind.

Roland said nothing and made no movement. He sat rigid, his eyes fixed on the fireplace.

'Is there anything wrong, Uncle?'

Roland shook his head slowly but made no reply. He was in profile to Peter and the thin face with its prominent cheekbones was thrown into deeply sculptured shadow by the single harsh light in the ceiling.

Peter tried to keep a conversation going.

'It's odd, but the regulars in the pub were asking whether you knew about the discovery yet. How the dickens they knew themselves, I'll never fathom. They knew as much about it as me – and I was with the doctor and Griffith when they found the stuff.'

This made Roland lift his head from the fire. He turned slowly and stared at his nephew.

'Oh, so they've started already, have they, boy?' he said in a curious flat voice. 'I should never have come back – I've felt it was a mistake all along.'

Peter looked at his uncle in alarm. He got up and stood over Roland, putting a hand comfortingly on his shoulder.

The old man patted the hand, then got wearily up from the chair.

'Don't ask me what's wrong, boy. Not tonight, anyway. There'll be plenty of time to find out – too much time, if I know Tremabon,' he added bitterly.

Something in his tone stopped Peter from asking more questions. He felt sympathy and affection welling up as the old man shuffled slowly across to the door of the stone staircase in the corner of the kitchen. Suddenly he seemed smaller and more bowed. He appeared to have aged ten years in as many minutes.

'Are you sure you're all right?' Peter asked softly. 'Shall I make some tea for you?'

Roland shook his head again.

'No, boy – no. I'd have an early night, if I were you.

We may have a lot to face after tomorrow comes.'

With those cryptic words, he went wearily up the winding stairs.

Chapter Three

'I'll bet it's been a hell of a long time since this spot saw so many people before, Peter!'

The morning breeze ruffled the dark hair of the speaker as he offered a packet of Players around the little group clustered at the mouth of the old lead mine.

'You missed the first act of the drama last night, David,' replied the journalist. 'Your father only needed one of those tweed caps to be the complete Sherlock Holmes!'

David Ellis-Morgan grinned at the thought of his father, whom he so much resembled, playing the detective.

'I can well imagine him, Peter! But he's had his share of the sensation – so Gerry and I left him to do morning surgery while we came up to have a snoop around.'

He turned and tapped his brother on the shoulder. Gerald was peering into the shaft, trying to make out what was happening amongst the flickering lights at the other end. 'See anything in there, Gerry?'

'There's only a lot of milling around, and a lot of cursing,' replied Gerald. He straightened up and accepted a cigarette from his brother's packet. Though he was the same build and had dark hair like David, his features were very different. He had the pointed Ellis-Morgan jaw, but there the likeness finished. He lit up and moved across to the bottom of the ramp, where three shirt-sleeved policemen sat resting on the grass.

'What exactly is going on in there, chaps?' asked Gerry in the hail-fellow-well-met manner that came so easily to him. 'From the entrance, it looks a real shambles!'

One of the policemen, brought by the CID to help with the manual work, pulled himself up and mopped his forehead, still sweating from his spell of excavating at the bottom of the shaft.

'Well, Doctor, our shift – that's us three – spent all our time just moving damn great stones from a heap and stacking them back along the passage. I don't know what the other boys are doing in there at the moment.'

Another of the constables spoke up.

'Hardly room to move in there, what with three of us, the superintendent, two inspectors and a sergeant – not to mention the photographer.'

'About ninety per cent policemen and ten per cent air, eh?' Gerry was addicted to facetious comments – in contrast to his more serious-minded brother, who was rather dour in his speech.

'What's been found so far?' asked Peter, his mind on the *Morning News*.

The police officer appeared to have read his thoughts. 'I really couldn't say, sir,' he replied evasively. 'But I think Superintendent Pacey picked up a few things.' Peter looked away from the mine entrance up to the crest of the grassy slopes above them. Here PC Griffith stood yawning after his night's vigil, keeping a small group of curious sightseers at bay.

'Wonderful where they come from, isn't it?' said one of the constables, following his gaze. 'If you had a corpse in the middle of the Sahara, there'd be a crowd of damn rubbernecks there inside ten minutes!'

Peter agreed fervently. 'It beats me how they knew about this in the village last night. Dash it, not two hours after we left here, I called in the pub, and they told me more about the affair than I knew myself!'

David gave a short laugh, tinged with annoyance.

'It's that ruddy woman in the post office – she knows the medical history of most of my patients better than I do

34

myself.'

A thoughtful expression came into Peter's face.

'Talking of this, there was some funny backchat in the Lamb about my uncle and these remains. I couldn't make head nor tail of it. But when I mentioned it to old Roland, he acted most oddly. He's not right even this morning – won't say anything – but I can tell that he's upset. Have you any ideas, Gerry? You've got your fingers on the local pulses – in more ways than one.'

The younger of the doctor brothers looked blankly at Peter.

'Sorry, not the faintest. But the gang that get into the Lamb of a night have always got some damn silly yarn to spin.'

'What about you, David. Any idea what the mystery is?'

David shook his head. He dropped his gaze and began fumbling with a cigarette.

'No – no, I've no idea, I'm sorry,' he said rather shortly.

Before Peter had time to speculate on the lack of conviction in the doctor's voice, there was a crunching of boots from inside the entrance of the shaft. A figure emerged blinking into the morning sunlight.

He was a thickset man, with a bull neck and shoulders like a wrestler. Though actually quite tall, his barrel-like body seemed to take inches off his height.

Peter had met him when he had asked permission to come up at eight o'clock; and he was able to introduce him to the Ellis-Morgan brothers as Detective-Superintendent Pacey, the CID officer in charge of the investigation.

Gerry immediately taxed him with one of his flippant remarks.

'What's going on down at the jaws of hell, there, Super?'

Charles Pacey rubbed a handkerchief over his chubby

face to remove the sweat and mud splashes.

'Looks like Hades too, Doc,' he said cheerfully, 'Still, the boys have done well; they've moved all the big rock already. It's just a question of scratching through the rubble and sieving some of it now.'

Pacey had a strong Welsh accent, but of the South Wales valleys, not the Cardigan twang. His bass voice suited his burly shape to perfection. He turned to the three men still sitting on the grass.

'Give them another quarter of an hour, then go in and let 'em have a break. OK?'

'But what have you found, Super?' persisted Gerald.

The detective grinned at him and deliberately prolonged the suspense.

'If you're Dr Gerald Ellis-Morgan, then you must be our police surgeon, sir.'

Gerry shrugged his shoulders and laughed.

'I am, in theory. But, in practice, it means that I have a look at a couple of drunks every year, that's all.'

Pacey beamed. Peter thought that his outward good humour was an effective way of covering his dealings with any unwary suspect. Beneath the benign 'farmer's boy' manner, the journalist sensed a flinty shrewdness.

'Well, here's your chance, Doc!' went on the detective. 'You can have first crack at this lot.'

He waved a ham-like hand at the entrance, where another raincoated figure was emerging, his arms full of polythene bags.

'Bring 'em over here, Willie,' Pacey said to his colleague – a tall, emaciated detective-inspector.

Willie Rees carried his load over to the spot that Pacey had pointed out and dumped them at the side of a photographer's holdall and a large wicker pannier, which stood on the grass.

The superintendent took a large plastic sheet from the

pannier, which was the 'Major Incident' box of the CID. It contained all sorts of bags and bottles, protective sheets and gadgets that could prove useful at the scene of a crime.

'We'll spread the stuff out on this, Willie. Now, Doctor, could you tell me something about this little lot?'

Pacey crouched by the sheet and spread the plastic bags on it. Each one had a luggage label tied around the neck, recording the exact site where the contents had been found. As he began undoing the strings on the bags, the others clustered around to get a good view.

Pacey suddenly twisted his head around to look at Peter.

'Mr Adams, I'm sure you'll remember your promise and not write anything for your paper without asking me first, eh?'

Peter agreed readily. He was too grateful for the chance of being present at all, to abuse his privilege. He watched the superintendent slide some brown fragments from the first bag.

'What about this, Doc?' the big man asked heartily.

There appeared to Peter to be several chunky pieces, and a few thin curved bones which even he recognized as ribs. Gerald picked up some bits, and David took the rest:

'These are vertebrae – bits of the spinal column,' pronounced the younger brother. 'My God, they look old to me! I wonder if we've got another Piltdown Man?'

'In a lead mine?' Pacey countered sweetly.

David was seriously staring at all sides of the bits which he had taken. 'These are ribs and a broken shoulder blade. Heaven only knows what the small bits belong to – could be fingers, I suppose.'

Peter thought again how like the father David was. His small eyes flickered behind his spectacles, and he had the same pointed chin that stuck out rather aggressively. David was two years older than his brother, and, in his thirty-four years, had picked up many of John Ellis-Morgan's

mannerisms.

Pacey looked up at David, squinting into the sun. 'So they are all human, without a doubt?'

'All the big pieces, certainly. I can't vouch for the scraps, though I should think that they are fragments knocked off the larger bones.'

The detective went carefully through the six bags of bones, showing the contents to the doctors and putting them back gently into their labelled containers.

'We've got a sketch plan of where all these were found, Willie, haven't we?'

The thin, nervous-looking inspector wagged his head.

'Yes, and photographs of each zone marked out on the floor.'

'Don't suppose it'll matter a damn, anyway,' Pacey said happily

'What's this zone business, Superintendent?' asked Peter.

'Oh, just a rough guide to record where each exhibit came from on the floor of the shaft. There's been such a devil of a fall of roof in there that it will bear no resemblance to the original position of the skeleton. But we'd better do it, just in case, I suppose.'

David and Gerald gave their opinion on as many of the bones as they could recognize and then abandoned the attempt. Pacey hauled himself elephantinely to his feet. Peter was struck by his resemblance in size to Ceri Lloyd, though his bulk looked all muscle instead of fat.

'Now then, gentlemen, can I have a couple of answers. First, this is a human skeleton – right?'

David looked seriously at the detective.

'Well, part of one, to be accurate.'

'How much is missing?'

'We've got no skull. And no legs below the knees.' said Gerry.

Pacey pulled his ear – a movement which Peter soon

came to recognize as sign of deep thought on the superintendent's part.

'Well, there's quite a bit of. stuff still to be sorted through.' He swung around to the resting policemen.

'Better get in there now, lads, and give the others a breather.'

As the men trooped into the dark hole, Pacey carried on with his questions.

'The next thing is – how many bodies?'

David's eyebrows went up. 'How many? One, of course!'

Pacey beamed again. Peter felt that if the big man were an executioner, he would smile as he sprung the trap.

'With respect, Doc, it isn't "of course". Are there any bones duplicated – have I got to look for the owners of one body – or two?'

David looked at Gerald for support.

'What d'you think, Gerry – were there too many of anything?'

'The bits are in such a tatty state that only an anatomist could be certain – it must be as old as hell!' Gerald seemed to be determined to push the deceased back at least into the Middle Ages.

'Right, then – next question. Male or female?'

Again the two practitioners looked doubtfully at one another.

'The pelvis – the hip bones – seem to be here, answered David. But they're smashed in pieces.'

'And there's no skull – so the two main parts for sexing it are missing,' added his brother.

David stood staring at the heap of plastic bags.

'What about it, Gerry? You've got a fifty-fifty chance of being right.'

'And an equal chance of making a fool of myself, too. Still, Dad said that he'd stuck his neck out last night and called it female, so we may as well back him up.'

David nodded his agreement and pushed his horn-rims back up his nose. Peter was reminded yet again of Ellis-Morgan senior.

Pacey peeled off his mud-spattered mackintosh to display a blue pinstriped suit.

'Too damn hot in that! Now, sirs, you're doing very well,' he complimented them. 'Ready for the jackpot question? How old is she? And how long has she been in there?'

David threw up his hands in mock horror.

'Would you like her name as well, Mr Pacey? You'll have to get your pathologist to answer that one – and good luck to him!'

'Has it been there six months, six years, or six hundred?' Pacey persisted gently.

'Certainly not the first two!' Gerald snapped, with professional indignation.

'No, I agree,' said his more-cautious brother. 'But I think the last one – six hundred – a bit much.'

'Oh, I don't know. Why not?' demanded Gerald.

'Because it would hardly be in the lead mine, if it was that old,' cut in Peter.

'Ah, that's cheating – I meant from the medical point of view,' replied Gerry.

'I don't give a damn how we find out,' said Pacey. 'If that's a good enough reason for scrubbing out the six hundred, fair enough. What about sixty instead?'

David shrugged. 'No good asking me, Superintendent, I haven't a clue – coughs and bellyache are my line of medicine.'

Pacey doggedly produced more questions. 'Any idea how old she was?'

Gerald Ellis-Morgan hooted scornfully.

'You've been watching too much television, Mr Pacey. The sort of programmes where the doctor feels the head of the corpse and says "He died at midnight – three weeks,

last Friday."!'

Pacey grinned even wider.

'I know the sort of thing you mean. They get me hopping mad, too. But I thought there might be something obvious that might give a lead to the age of the bones.'

'But surely, you're going to get somebody *really* expert to look at the stuff, aren't you?' asked David, a hint of exasperation in his voice.

'Oh yes. But, as you were here, I thought I'd get a bit of advance information.'

'Who's going to *be* the expert?' Gerald asked curiously.

'Professor Leighton Powell – from the medical school at Swansea.'

'Who's he – I seem to have heard the name?' Gerry had qualified in London and knew less about the local pundits than did his brother, who had trained in Wales.

'He's the Professor of Forensic Medicine and the local Home Office pathologist. I've heard him lecture.'

'He should be up later this morning,' explained Pacey.

'Well, David and I have shot our forensic bolt – so you'll have to leave your questions for him. And even the great experts will have their work cut out to learn much from this collection of antiques!' Gerald jerked a thumb at the heap of pathetic remains on the ground.

David looked pointedly at his wristwatch.

'Gerry, we've a day's work ahead of us, so we'd better get moving. Thanks for letting us see the stuff, Superintendent.'

Pacey thanked them in turn for their help and they set off across the turf towards the path down to Carmel House.

Before following them, Peter Adams turned to Pacey.

'Can I send just a few words off to my paper? I'm supposed to be on holiday. But, being on the spot like this, it is too much of a temptation.'

Charles Pacey looked blandly at the tall journalist.

'Very well, but just make it a short statement of the facts, will you. Nothing about the saw cut yet. And no fancy stuff about country-wide manhunts and imminent arrests!'

Peter hurried after the two brothers, being intent on telephoning the *Morning News* offices and scrounging a cup of coffee from his fiancée.

The detective-superintendent turned back to his lanky assistant. Willie Rees, although tall, had the advantage of not looking like a policeman. He could dissolve into any crowded place without arousing the suspicions of the most watchful crook.

'We'd better get back into that damn hole, Willie – here's the other shift coming out.'

Another trio of perspiring diggers trudged out of the entrance, to have a well-earned rest outside.

'Keep an eye on that lot of Nosy Parkers,' advised Pacey, pointing to the skyline where Griffith still kept a dozen snoopers at bay.

He stooped and plunged into the dark shaft, fumbling a torch from his pocket as he entered. With Rees close behind him, he shuffled down to the far end of the tunnel.

Inspector Morris, the uniformed man from Aberystwyth, was directing the efforts of the excavators. A detective-sergeant was waiting to take charge of any more finds; and a police photographer stood ready with his flash-camera at one side.

'Well done, Morris, not much left now,' said Pacey.

Morris, dressed in a suit of dungarees, shone his hand lamp on the side wall of the shaft.

'I'm beginning to wonder what that is up there,' he said.

Pacey picked up another powerful electric lamp from the floor and directed it at the wall.

'You mean that shelf affair up there?'

'Yes, it's right up against the old working face – looks

as if they started to cut a side gallery, then gave it up.'
Pacey saw that about six feet from the ground, there was a
rough ledge running back from the blind end of the
working for a few yards. It was covered with loose stones;
and, above it, the beam of the light vanished into a black
cavern in the roof.

'I'm wondering if these bones might have been on that
ledge originally,' suggested Morris. He was an oldish man,
humourless and severe, although quite an efficient officer,
as far as Pacey knew.

The superintendent looked hard at the shelf.

'Yes, could quite well have been,' he agreed. 'And that
fall of roof might have swept it off onto the floor, eh?'
Rees waggled his own torch to draw attention to the rocks
which lay on the nearer end of the ledge.

'Those stones look as if they've been stacked there
deliberately. They're covered in slime – not like the ones
that have fallen out of the roof.'

Pacey looked closely and saw that half a dozen big
stones were stacked tidily at the end of the ledge, like
bricks in a wall.

'Nip up and have a look, Willie. You're the tallest. Get
on Edward's back.'

The inspector hoisted himself onto the shoulders of one
of the more burly constables and peered over the barrier of
stones on the shelf, his head up in the cavity in the roof.

'Have a few of these big 'uns down there, will you.' He
passed a few large rocks down to waiting hands and thrust
his hand lamp over the rubble.

There was a moment's silence.

'Ugh! For Christ's sake, let me down!'

Willie Rees slid to the floor more quickly than he had
gone up. Even in the poor light, his face could be seen to
be paler than usual.

'What's up there?' demanded the detective-
superintendent.

43

'At one end there's a head – a skull, rather. And, down the bottom, there's a pair of legs with sort of waxy flesh on them and the bones sticking up out of the middle, They look bloody horrible!' His lips pulled back in an expression of revulsion.

Pacey turned a satisfied face to the dour Morris.

'You were dead right, then. That's where it came from.'

The constable who had supported Rees offered to climb up and get the remains from the ledge.

'No, hang on a bit, we'd better get a photo first, before we shift them.'

Whilst the photographer was doing contortions in order to get a record of the gruesome discovery, Pacey discussed its significance with the inspectors.

'It's getting to look nasty, isn't it? What do you think about it, Morris?'

'Must be murder, surely – no other reason for such an elaborate hiding place, and that's apart from that saw cut.'

Pacey rubbed his bristly chin.

'Looks like it, I'll admit. Certainly can't be accident or suicide. And I can't see anyone going to all this trouble just to get rid of a body that died of natural causes. The only point now is: when did all this happen? If this is some flaming Roman, or even mid-Victorian, corpse, it's no concern of ours. The coroner can amuse himself with it, if he likes, but there's no possibility of charging anyone if it's older than, say, fifty years.'

His train of thought was broken by an exclamation from one of the constables who was clearing the rubble beneath the ledge.

'Something here, Super!'

As the others bent down and focused their torches, the PC carefully removed a tarnished piece of metal from the pile of debris.

'Looks like brass – yes, it's the clasp of an old purse,

sir.' He displayed it on the palm of his hand, a bent strip of metal, hinged at each end, covered with a green coating of verdigris.

'Watch how you handle it,' ordered Pacey. 'Sergeant, have you got another plastic bag?'

While the find was being carefully wrapped, Morris moved some more small stones from the same area of floor.

'Here we are, some more. Looks like finger bones. And here's a ring, by damn!'

Pacey watched him fish out a wide gold band. Immediately, his eyes were caught by more metal lower down in the hole that Morris had made.

'And there are some coins, too. We've struck it rich this time!'

He reached into the cavity and delicately picked out a coin, holding it by its edges.

Pacey gazed at the corroded brown surface for a moment. Then he looked up at the faces of the other policemen, who were staring at him expectantly.

'Well, we can forget our Romans – *and* our Victorians! This penny has the head of George V on it!'

Chapter Four

'This stuff is called "adipocere". It's near enough to being soap as makes little difference.'

The speaker prodded the pallid fat of a disintegrating leg which was lying before him on an enamel tray.

Professor Powell seemed to be enjoying himself. Apart from the rubber gloves on his hands, he looked more like a successful stockbroker having a chat at his club than a coroner's pathologist at work.

'What exactly does that mean?' asked Charles Pacey, who was seated on the other side of John Ellis-Morgan's consulting room desk. The little doctor had offered them the use of his surgery for the afternoon, so that the Home Office man could study the remains in comparative comfort. Leighton Powell began to explain:

'It forms when the body is exposed to a lot of damp – the fats are changed to a kind of soap. This change is permanent, as far as I know. It lasts for many years, anyway – unless rats come and eat it, which is quite common.'

Pacey looked a little disappointed.

'So it doesn't help to time the date of death?'

'No, only that it must be at least a few months since death, it doesn't happen in a shorter time than that.'

Pacey looked with revulsion at the two decaying legs lying on the white tray.

'I was hoping that the persistence of flesh meant that death couldn't have taken place more than a short time ago.'

'It isn't really flesh,' explained the pathologist. 'It's

only the fat – the actual flesh has gone long ago.'

The detective abandoned the subject and started on another.

'Well, Professor, you've seen all the stuff we've got – and you've been up to the mine yourself. Everything we've found is on those trays.'

He waved at another pair of white surgical trays belonging to the surgery, on which were heaped the polythene bags full of trophies from the shaft.

'So if we could have a quick recap, I can get some sort of preliminary story ready for my chief constable. He's expecting me to ring him at about four o'clock, to tell him what the situation is.'

Pacey's mind was flying ahead to this telephone call. He knew from experience that the chief, an ex-infantry colonel, would expect a detailed account of the day's findings presented to him with military precision. In arriving at this summary for the police chief, Pacey was glad that he had such a sensible man as Powell to work with. He had known other pathologists who were either misleadingly dogmatic, or so woolly-headed that they could not be pinned down to any opinion, even if it was a firm 'I don't know'.

'What do you want to know first?' asked the professor cheerfully, polishing his glasses with a flourish of a dazzling white handkerchief.

'All about that lot,' requested Pacey, with a sweep of his great hand towards the heap of debris on the trays.

'Right-oh. One body, as far as I can tell now. I'll have to get the anatomy people to check on the small and broken stuff, but I don't think there's any duplication at all.'

'How much is missing?'

Powell pursed his lips. 'Mmm, very little, really. All the limb bones are there, though some are broken. The skull, pelvis and most of the spine are there. Probably some ribs and toe and finger bones are missing. But that's about all.'

Pacey nodded and scribbled on a piece of paper for the benefit of Colonel Barton. Then he looked up.

'The next thing is sex, Professor.'

Leighton Powell almost giggled. 'Yes; it usually is, Mr Pacey – even at my age. But seriously, that's easy here. Definitely a woman. I'll get the anatomy boys in Swansea to make dead sure. But there's almost no doubt at all; it's female all right.'

'And what about her age, sir?'

The doctor's eyes twinkled above his chubby pink cheeks. He had a round, almost babyish face, with a shiny, scrubbed look about it, which extended up to his polished pink bald head.

'Yes, Superintendent, that's an Eleven-plus question, isn't it! I can give you a definite age bracket now, but to narrow it down within that range will take a day or two. I'll have to get X-ray and other things to get as near as I can to the actual year.'

'And what's your bracket, Professor?'

'Definitely more than eighteen, and probably less than thirty-three.'

Pacey's face registered his disappointment. 'That's a pretty wide range, isn't it?'

Powell grinned at him. 'We can do a lot better than that eventually, but I don't want to mislead you at this stage. With X-rays and other dodges, we can get much closer than that. As it is, I'd put a couple of bob on her being somewhere in the middle or late twenties.'

'That's better,' Pacey said grudgingly. 'Now, what about her height and that sort of thing?'

The Home Office man held up a thigh bone, the one found by the boys on the previous day.

'She was five foot four, give or take an inch either way.'

'How can you tell from just a leg bone?' Willie Rees asked curiously. He sat on the examination couch, along with Inspector Meadows, the liaison officer from the Forensic Science laboratory in Swansea.

'There are special calculations for it, worked out years ago from hundreds of bodies – one of these "double it and take away the number you first thought of" efforts! Again, I'll have it checked by the anatomy department when I get back to the University. But five foot four will be pretty near her true height, I'm sure.'

Pacey scribbled away on his pad before shooting the next question.

'Now, sir, how long would you say that the body has been in the shaft?'

Powell chuckled. 'If you'd asked me that before you showed me those pennies, I'd have said that I hadn't the faintest idea. But, as I've seen them, I'll say thirty years!'

Pacey grinned sheepishly in his turn. 'I suppose I should have kept those up my sleeve, shouldn't I? But seriously, what's the medical angle on the time of death?'

'Anything from two years to two hundred. I was going to say two thousand – but I think, on second thoughts, that they are too well-preserved for that. There is still a lot of organic matrix in the bones. They would be dry and crumbly if they were really ancient.'

'Two years!' echoed Inspector Meadows incredulously. 'Can they get that bad in such a short time?'

Powell nodded. 'I've seen a body converted completely to a skeleton – clean as a whistle – in eight months. That was out in the open, I'll admit, with bugs and birds and mice after it. But, even in a cave like this, I'd say it could happen in a couple of years. It was very wet there, remember, and there would be a lot of contaminated surface water seeping through from the ground not far overhead.'

Pacey spread his hands out in an almost French gesture.

'Well, as it happens, it doesn't matter much – we've got all this other evidence. But can you say, Professor, that the state of the body is consistent with thirty years' burial?'

'Yes, quite definitely,' Powell said firmly.

'Any clue as to the cause of death?' asked the superintendent.

'Not a chance, Mr Pacey. All the organs and soft tissues have gone, except these bits of leg. No skin left – nothing. Unless there was a bullet hole in one of the bones, no form of violence would leave any signs on a heap of junk like this.'

Pacey leaned forward and picked up the brown skull. 'What about these holes in the top.'

Powell brushed a speck of dirt from his city suit and smiled sadly.

'Sorry, nothing doing. There's nothing about those fractures that could tell me they were done before death. In fact, from the size and shape of them, I'd be inclined to say that they were due to a load of rock falling down on the head.'

Pacey sighed and put the skull down.

'Anything else you can tell me at present, sir?'

Powell rubbed a palm over his bald head as though he were polishing it.

'I don't think so,' he said with studied care. 'Even what I've said now is provisional, most of it. I'll need a long session with the anatomy boys, and some time to myself back at the department, to clinch the facts.'

'You're taking all this stuff back with you this afternoon, then?'

'Yes, all the bits of body, anyway. The other stuff is Inspector Meadows' pigeon.'

Pacey turned to the man from the Home Office laboratory, an oldish inspector with slicked-back white hair. His function was to act as the link between the scene of crimes and the actual scientific work. 'I'd better get my story word-perfect for the chief,' Pacey said wryly. 'Otherwise, he'll have me doing fatigues as if he was still running his damn battalion. Now, Meadows, what have we got there altogether?'

The liaison officer went through his list and checked it against the collection of plastic bags, cellophane envelopes and glass jars, all of which were neatly labelled.

'Clasp of an old-fashioned purse, no fabric left on it. Five coins – a florin, shilling and three pennies – all dated from nineteen twelve to nineteen twenty-seven. A narrow, plain gold wedding ring, with hallmarks.'

Meadows paused while he peered through some of the bags to see what was inside.

'Oh, yes, this is hair – in a devil of a mess, mixed up with mud and slime. But it looks brownish-red in colour.'

'I'd like to have a look at a bit of that, if I can,' asked the pathologist.

Meadows handed him a small polythene packet.

'You can have this, sir. I divided the hair into three lots.'

'What else have you got?' persevered the superintendent, being intent upon finishing his aide-mémoire.

'This big bag has got parts of the skirt – looks like a skirt to me – linen, I would say. This one is the remains of a blouse. There are a couple of pearl buttons on it and a few lines of embroidered stitching.'

Pacey scratched away in his notebook.

'A couple of pieces of shoe in here,' went on Meadows. 'Pointed toe and a strap over the instep. No soles left, but they'd do all right for the styles of the Roaring Twenties, from what I remember of them.'

Leighton Powell reached out for the bag and inspected the pathetic remnants of shoe.

'Looks exactly like the blasted things my teenage daughter wears now – "winkle-pickers" they call 'em, don't they?'

'What's in those little bags there?' demanded Pacey. 'I've lost track of where half the stuff was put.'

'This one is a broken necklace; gilt-on-brass chain, by the looks of it. This one is a hair-clip, with another bit of hair still stuck in it – a definite reddish colour this time.'

'Anything else?'

'Um, just these. Three big wooden beads, pretty rotten, and half a dozen glass ones.'

'And that's the lot?''

'Yes – unless the boys up on the cliff have found any more by sieving the last of the muck on the floor.'

Pacey looked at his watch.

'Morris should be down soon. He said they would finish by half two, or three. Oh, I forgot one thing, Professor. What about the teeth? I seem to remember that they have been important in many identification problems in the past.'

Powell looked ruefully at the detective.

'They certainly are important – but this girl's are a wash-out. Though if you ever get a possible candidate for this body, even the negative evidence might help.'

'Why is it such a dead loss here?'

'All the teeth that are left in the jaws are perfectly healthy – no fillings or extractions – so that it's unlikely that any dental records exist anywhere to give a clue as to the owner.'

'You said "the teeth that are left". Where are the others?'

The doctor shrugged.

'God only knows – they're missing from the sockets. They tend to come loose after death and fall out. Perhaps your men will find a few in their sieves, if we're lucky – not that it will help much, unless there's some dental work done on them.'

Pacey looked at his watch again.

'I'd better ring the Old Man, I suppose. I expect Miss Ellis-Morgan would let me use her phone to save me from going all the way over to the police house.'

The burly policeman got up and went to the door. He turned and made a last appeal to the pathologist and laboratory man.

'So there's no more you can tell me? This is the skeleton of a woman in her middle, or late, twenties. No cause of death apparent, but one arm partly sawn through. The clothing, ornaments and coins suggest that she died in the nineteen twenties or early thirties. Is that right?'

There was a murmur of assent and Pacey left the surgery to telephone the chief constable – who insisted upon being informed personally of any serious crimes in the county.

Colonel Barton seemed to be quite impressed by the results of the first few hours' investigation. Pacey was pleasantly surprised at the lack of searching questions which the 'Old Man' usually fired at him on these occasions.

He went back to the surgery and helped Powell and Meadows to load the remains into the professor's Jaguar, which stood outside the front door of Carmel House. The pathologist was taking Meadows back to Swansea and Pacey waited on the drive to see them leave.

'I'll let you know as soon as I get any more gen,' Powell called through the window as he let in the clutch. 'Probably be tomorrow afternoon.'

The car moved off, the boot stuffed with the last mortal remains of the unknown young woman.

Morris had not yet come down from the cliff with his digging team and Pacey decided to go up and meet him. He looked up from the garden at the steep cliff path opposite and wished that he were a few stone lighter.

With a sigh, he set off; but, as he reached the gate, a blue-uniformed figure came down the lane from the village, perched on a tall bicycle.

PC Griffith squeaked to a halt in front of the detective, hopped off and saluted.

'Excuse me, Super, I hope I'm not speaking out of turn. But, living in the village, like, I thought I'd better let you know.'

Pacey stared at him. He had never met Griffith before that day, but had sized him up as a sensible, reliable man.

'That's all right. What's on your mind?'

Wynne looked a little embarrassed.

'Well, it's only village gossip, see, but the place is buzzing with it today. I should have known earlier, but I was up on the cliff all night.'

Pacey nodded his understanding and waited for the police constable to come to the point. He knew only too well that no outside detective could know the feeling of the district as well as the bobby on the spot.

'It's the old people, sir. They're putting the poison about. First I've ever heard of it, see – I was in my cradle when this happened.'

Griffith leant over his handlebars towards the superintendent and spoke earnestly for five minutes.

There was some discussion. Then he jumped back on to his ponderous machine and rode back towards the village, leaving a very thoughtful detective staring after him.

Chapter Five

In spite of Peter Adams being involved right at the outset of the affair, it was his uncle who heard the first accusing whispers from the village.

Peter had stayed to lunch at Carmel House. If any of the doctors had picked up any scandal on their morning rounds, they kept it to themselves.

By the time he got back to the cottage at teatime, he found that his uncle had had two callers, both of whom were assuming that Roland already knew of the gossip.

The first was the postman, who went up with the late delivery. He was too young to have remembered the thirty-year-old scandal, but he had made up for it on his early round that morning.

The second caller was the dairyman from Aberystwyth, who came twice a week to collect eggs from Roland's poultry. He had picked up the gist of the story from his other calls, like the postman. Both of them were quite ready to talk about it with the old man, but they found him brusque and short-tempered, quite unlike his usual self. Both the men were also openly incredulous about the whole business; and the dairyman, in particular, thought it a big joke. Roland refused to be drawn into saying anything more than a curt 'damn nonsense', so the men had to leave without gleaning any more juicy bits to pass on to their next calls.

When Peter got back, he found his uncle sitting by the kitchen fire, poking it with unusual ferocity. The dog was crouched in a corner of the room, head on one side, looking warily at his master. Once again, Peter sensed that something was radically wrong with his usually placid uncle.

Roland threw the poker into the fender with unnecessary violence.

'Peter boy, have you been into the village?'

'No. I've been down with Mary most of the day – since early this morning, anyway. Why d'you ask?'

Roland Hewitt jumped out of his chair and went to the window. He stood staring out at the paved yard and garden beyond, his back to his nephew. Peter noticed that he hadn't bothered to shave, or even put on a collar and tie.

'So you haven't heard the talk, eh?'

His voice was harsh and his fingers trembled as he passed them through the grey stubble of his hair. He turned and began to pace up and down, until Peter stood in his path to block his agitated wandering.

'Look here,' began Peter. 'There's something worrying you, isn't there? Something to do with these blasted bones?'

Roland stared up at him, then seemed to crumple. His thin body drooped and went as limp as a punctured tyre.

'Sit down there, boy, and listen.' He sank back wearily into his own big chair and stared into the embers of the fire that he had just wrecked.

'I may as well tell you the whole story now. You'll be hearing it soon enough from other places, no doubt.'

Peter stayed silent, letting the old man feel his way.

'I don't know how much your mother told you about my affairs. But, knowing the family, I expect they did their best to keep it quiet.'

That's true enough, thought his nephew. When he was a child, Uncle Roland had been a name that the grown-ups used to whisper in front of the young ones.

To them, he was the black sheep who had gone to Canada. Any questions about him from the children were either ignored or evaded with such persistence that, eventually, he came to be a legend on a par with Santa Claus.

Peter's mother kept up a sporadic correspondence with Roland; but the rest of the family elders seemed to have denied his existence.

'Your mother was the only one who ever had any time for me, bless her! She was the only one who bothered with me after I came back – apart from you, boy.'

Roland spoke in a dull monotone, staring into the ashes.

'I shouldn't have come back. But I wanted to see the old place and have a few years here before I went.'

He slipped back into speaking Welsh and Peter followed suit.

'What's this got to do with the gossip you're on about?' he asked, gently trying to prompt his uncle to get to the point.

'They're saying in Tremabon that this body up on the cliff is that of my wife – your Aunt Mavis,' he said bleakly. 'That I killed her all those years back and hid her up there.'

Peter experienced a curious sensation. He knew that he should be appalled and shocked, yet he realized that this was what he must have been expecting. He had connected the two events, the bones and his uncle's strangeness, in his subconscious mind; but only now had Roland's bald statement thrust it into the front of his thoughts.

His knowledge of his aunt was almost nil – he had been brought up to accept the fact that she had 'run away' from Uncle Roland, but the hint was left that he was not all that blameless himself. The whole affair was one of the unmentionable subjects in the family, like sex and cancer. He and his sisters had been brainwashed from infancy not to have any interest in it.

'But that's absurd – ridiculous!'

He heard himself speak the words and realized how banally inadequate they were.

Roland, now that he had started, plunged on with his story:

'I was a lot older than Mavis when we married. That was another mistake, like coming back here to live. She was pretty – by Heaven she was! – but she was a bitch. A real little bitch, boy! We fought all the time, me trying to keep her respectable and her laughing in my face.'

Peter saw his uncle's bony fists clenching and opening spasmodically as his mind flew back over the years. His thin face was grey with anguish at the memories.

'We stuck it for the best part of two years. Then things came to a head, and she went. God only knows where to. I never saw her again.'

'Why did you quarrel so much?'

'She was a little tart. I should have seen that long before I ever married her, I suppose.' Roland replied bitterly. 'But I was as silly an old fool then as I am now. I was too flattered to realize it, but of course she only married me to get out of working as a parlourmaid. I was left the farm by my uncle when I was thirty. So I was a good catch for a girl in service in those days – she made herself mistress of a hundred acres freehold. But that wasn't all she was mistress of, not by a long way.'

'Does Ceri Lloyd come into this, by any chance?' Peter asked quietly.

His uncle nodded. 'Indeed, he does. He was the main cause of the trouble – though, to be fair, if it hadn't been him, there would have been someone else in the village. She would have found another man to amuse herself with. I found out, afterwards that they had been pretty thick before we got married. And she didn't let the wedding stop her fun. Ceri wasn't well off enough for her to want to marry him instead of me – he worked in his father's shop then, long before he had the Lamb and Flag.'

'So the cause of the trouble between you was her carrying on with Lloyd?' concluded Peter.

'That was one part of it – but there were other men besides him, I'm sure. She took to going home to Liverpool for weeks on end. I know she had a good time up there when she went, and she only came home when her money ran out. Then she'd be nice to me for a bit. And, like a fool, I'd fall for it.'

'And this went on for a couple of years?'

'Yes, almost as long as that. Getting worse all the time.'

'Why didn't you divorce her?'

Roland shrugged helplessly. 'In those days, "divorce" was a terrible word to people of our class. I'd married her for better or worse, in the chapel, and I thought I had to put up with it. Anyway, I didn't know how to go about it – though, just before she went, I was beginning to think about a separation, if not actual divorce, boy.'

'What happened eventually – and how on earth does this body come into it, for goodness' sake?'

'Towards the end, she was going off to Liverpool even more often. She wouldn't say anything, she'd just vanish and I wouldn't see her for perhaps a month. She'd say she'd been staying with her sister, if she bothered to tell me anything at all. But, for all I know, she could have been anywhere in the country. A real bad one, she was! God knows, I was only a dull old farmer, but I did my best to please her when we got married.'

His voice cracked with emotion. 'I reckon I loved her then, but I came to hate her before those couple of years were past.'

Peter could see the old man's pale eyes moistening behind his old-fashioned glasses. He hurriedly changed the subject.

'But what about her actual disappearance – why should there be all that nonsense about her being dead?'

'The last few months were worse than ever, boy. She would come home from Liverpool, or from being with

Lloyd, and start fighting right away – real fighting, shouting, screaming, kicking – everything! She even came at me with a knife once, in her temper – saying how I'd ruined her life and was keeping her short of everything. It was terrible!'

Roland rose abruptly from the fireside and began pacing the floor again.

'I started hitting her back in the end – partly to keep her off me. She used to go mad with rage. But, in the end, it was hate and temper on my part, too – God forgive me!'

Peter heard his uncle's voice tremble. He had never before seen him in anything other than his usual placid and rather vague state of mind. The change was disturbing, almost frightening; and Peter was suddenly afraid that the old man was going to break down altogether.

'But what actually happened at the end?' he persisted, trying to stem the flood of emotion by concentrating on fact.

Roland Hewitt stopped walking around and leant heavily on the edge of the kitchen table, staring down at the cloth.

'One day, she didn't come home. Must have been the middle of September, nineteen twenty-nine. There was nothing new in that. For a couple of weeks I thought she had gone on one of her trips to Liverpool. But then a letter came for her in her sister's handwriting, so I knew she couldn't be there. After another week, there was a second letter. Then, soon after, this sister – another bitch cast out of the same mould as Mavis herself – arrived on the doorstep demanding to know where Mavis was. Just about hysterical, she was.'

Peter's uncle paused as the scene flooded back into his mind.

'I didn't have any time for this sister and I told her so. I'd had about enough of Mavis's antics by then. I wasn't anxious to go hunting around the country, looking for her.

I thought she was probably with some man. The sister raised the roof. I sent her packing, and she went straight to the police in Aberystwyth – saying that I'd done away with my wife.'

Peter stared at Roland incredulously. 'But that's just plain ridiculous! Surely they didn't take any notice of a silly accusation like that.'

'It wasn't just her word, boy. I didn't know it then, but Mavis had been writing to her sister saying that she was going to leave me and that I was ill-treating her and injuring her and all the rest of it. The last time she went home, she showed some bruises to her.'

'What was the point of that?'

'I think she was working up to getting a divorce herself. She was a cunning little devil. She probably thought that, if she could divorce me for cruelty before I left her, she would get a good settlement and be free to carry on her affairs. Anyway, there were some letters as well, to this sister, which suggested that I was on the point of doing something drastic to her. Then that swine Ceri Lloyd went to the police with a lot of lies and made it worse still.'

'What happened then?'

'This sister had gone to the local paper in Aber and spun them the same yarn. They published an appeal for anyone who knew where Mavis was to contact them. Damn reporters came pestering me at Bryn Glas. Then the police came nosing around. A wonder I wasn't had up for turning a shotgun on someone, the trouble I had over those few weeks.'

'What did the police have to say to you?'

'I don't think they took it very seriously at the time. They sized up the sister and Ceri Lloyd. But they had to do something for the sake of appearances. They soon dropped it, though.'

'How long did all this trouble go on for?'

'Until I cleared off to Canada. Some Sunday paper got

hold of it – they must have been short of news in twenty-nine, because they took over where the local paper left off. They ran a big article about the "Mystery of Bryn Glas", silly fools! That kept the scandal going. The village all judged and condemned me, of course. That fat swine Lloyd was the mouthpiece – he joined forces with the sister and went round talking to the reporters whenever he had the chance.'

'You could have had him for slander, surely?' Peter said indignantly.

Roland sighed and shuffled back to his chair, his lean face grey and tired.

'I suppose so, boy, but I was too worried to care. Everywhere I went, I felt that people were whispering and pointing at me – "Look, there's the man who murdered his wife." I stuck it for a couple of months, and then I had a chance of a quick sale for the farm. So, almost overnight, I sold up and went over to Alberta. I knew a fellow from Tremabon who had settled there, and he helped me get settled in a job in an agricultural store there. It wasn't a bad life. I did pretty well over the years, but I always pined for the old place.'

Roland looked around the kitchen as if he were seeing it for the first time.

'I could have finished up here quite well, boy, but you can't get away from the past.'

Peter leant forward and spoke earnestly to the old man.

'You've got nothing to get away from, Uncle! There's nothing in what you've just told me to cause you to get upset and worried like this. Only a few old fools in the village shooting their mouths off. If they dare say anything that I can pin onto any particular person, we'll get a lawyer to teach them a lesson!'

Roland Hewitt stared at his nephew with troubled eyes. 'I don't know, boy – I just don't know. I feel that something bad is going to happen. I've got to dreading every knock on the door today.'

'Why, for goodness' sake? I don't need telling that you had nothing to do with Aunt Mavis's vanishing trick. What is there to be afraid of, then? You didn't kill your wife so this heap of bones in a cave is no concern of yours!'

Roland refused to be reassured. 'They're all saying in the village that she was the only woman to be missing from Tremabon in living memory, so this must be her.'

Peter groaned in exasperation.

'Look, that's nonsense! You know as well as I do that the skeleton can't be Mavis. You didn't put it there, and there's no reason why anyone else should have. That's all there is to it. Anyway, the state that thing is in, it could have been there for generations, so this must be the body of someone else. The police aren't fools, not by a hell of a long way. They'll be able to tell that this is the body of someone else in no time.'

The logic of this seemed to strike home at last. A more hopeful expression crept into Roland's face.

'You really think so, boy?'

Peter piled on the bedside manner. 'Of course. They have scientists these days who will make mincemeat of these rumours in the village. They may never be able to say exactly who the bones belong to, but I'll bet they know already that they can't possibly have come from Mavis Hewitt.'

Chapter Six

'Going on what the pathologist has told us so far, sir, there seems no reason why this couldn't be Mavis Hewitt.' With an air of finality, Pacey laid a thin folder on the edge of the chief constable's desk.

The detective-superintendent and his assistant sat in Colonel Barton's office on the first floor of the County Constabulary Headquarters at Cardigan. Following his talk with the local constable at Tremabon, Pacey had gone back up the cliff as fast as his bulk would allow him. He collected Willie Rees and the few more objects that the digging team had found amongst the last rubble in the shaft, then left Inspector Morris to organize the sealing-off of the tunnel.

He then hustled back with Rees to his police Wolseley and drove off rapidly towards Aberystwyth. After an hour of furious activity in the basement of the police station there, he had telephoned the chief, then roared away again down the coast road to Cardigan.

By the time they arrived in the county town, it was about seven o'clock in the evening of that strenuous Monday. Pacey was beginning to yearn for a rest and a decent meal. But, with Rees still in tow, he went straight to the police headquarters where the colonel was waiting for them. He gave him a succinct account of the day's events and ended up by sliding the pitifully thin file with its scanty record of the case, onto the desk.

'All I've got so far is in there, sir, but there's nothing important that I haven't already mentioned.'

The chief constable reached for it and carefully scanned

the few sheets of paper which it contained.

Inspector Rees sat primly on a hard chair at one end of the desk, looking like an elderly spinster at a vicar's tea party. Charles Pacey, his large body draped uncomfortably over another small chair at the opposite end of the desk, waited patiently for the chief to say something.

Colonel Barton sat bolt upright in his swivel chair, one hand fingering his neat grey toothbrush moustache as he studied the file.

He looked up at last. 'And you say, Superintendent, that there's no sign of the original report of the sister's complaint in the records at Aberystwyth?'

'No, sir. We had a good search through all the old records in the station. But, apart from an entry in the daily Occurrences book, there was nothing else.'

Willie Rees thought of the frantic hour they had just spent in the basement of the police station, scrabbling through heaps of dusty paper tied in even dirtier string.

'Do you think anything will turn up, either after a better search or, perhaps, here in the headquarters archives?'

Pacey looked doubtful. 'I haven't much hope of that, Colonel. Thirty years is a long time and the war in between played havoc with a lot of storage routines. I know tons of stuff was thrown out to make room for shelters and things like that.'

'Where can we hope to get some further information?' The colonel rapped out his questions in the manner of one with years of military command behind him.

Pacey, looking like a village yokel compared with the small, neat figure in front of him, puffed out his red cheeks as he considered this.

'Well, there's the local newspaper files. Their office in Aber was shut when I was there. So I thought it could wait until morning, without going chasing after the editor. Then we might find someone who was in the police force thirty years ago and might remember something about it. None of the present men up there are anything like old enough. But I've got the names of a couple of retired officers who might have been there at the time.'

'Then, of course, there's this sister. The one mentioned in the station report book.' The colonel deftly removed Pacey's trump card before he could play it.

'Yes, sir, I've already telexed the Liverpool police to see if she's still alive and at the same address,' said the detective, being determined to win the trick.

'We'll be lucky to find her after all this time – she must be getting on now.' Willie Rees diffidently threw his voice into the duet between Pacey and the chief.

Pacey shrugged his bull shoulders.

'It's still possible. Her age wasn't mentioned anywhere. But she sounds like an elder sister, judging by the way she was acting.'

The colonel carefully brushed up the ends of his military moustache. 'Then, of course, you'll have to get around the village people pretty thoroughly tomorrow.'

Pacey groaned silently. His chief was a good scout in that he would always back any of his men up to the hilt against outsiders; but he had this annoying habit of stating the obvious as if it were a stroke of his own genius.

'Er, yes, sir,' replied Pacey. 'I'll work them over first thing in the morning. I'll take Sergeant Mostyn with me as there's not much else doing to keep him here.'

'When will the scientific people be able to give you some really detailed information?'

'Professor Powell is taking all the bones to his anatomy department in the morning and he hopes to be able to let me know something over the phone later in the day. I expect that the Forensic Lab will be longer than that with the stuff they've got, though.'

'What did Morris's diggers unearth this afternoon – you said you collected some more things from him?'

'A few more beads, two teeth and some more hair –

again definitely reddish in colour. There were a few scraps of cloth and a bit more shoe, as well.'

'So there's plenty for the boffins to work on?' observed Barton, fiddling with his moustache again.

'Yes, sir, I've already sent it down to the Swansea lab.'

The colonel delicately adjusted the position of his inkstand and straightened up the already faultless blotting pad.

'The question is now, how much proof do we need before we tackle this chap Hewitt?'

Pacey scratched his thick red neck.

'It all hangs on the identity, doesn't it? If we can't get anywhere near showing that this heap of bones is Mavis, we can't even contemplate charging him. In fact, all we've got to go on, so far, is a load of village gossip.'

The chief frowned.

'The dates of those coins, and the type of clothing, are very suggestive, especially in a sparsely populated district such as this. It's not like London, thank God, where people are disappearing every few hours, you know.'

Pacey throttled back an impertinent answer. 'Yes, sir, I know that. But the slightest bit of contrary evidence will blow that one coincidence wide open. Someone might come along tomorrow and say that Mavis Hewitt was six foot tall, had blonde hair and a wooden leg!'

The chief constable gave Pacey a withering look of disapproval.

'That's hardly likely, is it, Superintendent?' he snapped.

The detective had a sudden mental flashback to his army days and for a brief moment felt as if he were standing between two redcaps in front of his CO.

'A bit overstated, perhaps,' he admitted. 'But the slightest variation between the skeleton and the real Mavis's description will be enough to flatten the whole theory. And that's all it is, so far – a tentative theory.'

'Are you going to have a talk with Hewitt tomorrow?'

'I certainly am. This is the sort of situation where a bit of shaking up can lead to a confession and save a hell of a lot of work. Especially with old jossers like Hewitt. Let him think we know everything – instead of damn all – and he might crumple up for us. That's if he knows anything at all about it, of course.'

The colonel looked uneasy.

'I hope you'll use your discretion, Pacey. You know how things are between the police and the public these days. Not that I'm trying to tell you your business. You know that I never interfere in my officers' work. All I want is to be kept in the picture.'

Charles Pacey sighed again. This was another well-known ploy of the chief's, declaring how he never meddled in the routine but just sat in the background like a benign father confessor.

'Is there anything else you'd like to discuss, sir?' Pacey looked pointedly at his watch.

'There's one thing, Pacey. You didn't tell me exactly what was in that report from the old station Occurrences book – it's the only written evidence we have so far.'

'It's in the file, sir – on the last page.'

The colonel opened the folder again and read aloud the copy that Rees had taken in Aberystwyth a few hours before.

'"October the eighth, nineteen twenty-nine ... Mrs Jessie Randall, 14 Speke Street, Liverpool, reported her sister, Mavis Hewitt, missing from Bryn Glas farm, Tremabon. Also made allegations against brother-in-law, Roland Hewitt of same address. Alleged missing woman is Mavis Cecily Hewitt, age twenty-six years. Case referred to Inspector Williams".'

The chief constable dropped the sheet and looked up at Pacey.

'Doesn't help much, does it?' he concluded.

'A case like that would be handled by the inspector from the start,' commented Pacey. 'He probably interviewed the sister and opened a special file – so there wouldn't be any more details in the Occurrences book.'

'And this Inspector Williams – what happened to him?'

'Retired and dead this many years, so I discovered.'

Barton pondered this for a moment. 'So, now, we have to wait to see what the pathologist, the "lab" and Hewitt have got to tell us, eh?'

'And check on all the missing persons around the late twenties and early thirties,' said Pacey, getting in ahead of the chief with the suggestion. 'As I said, this yarn about Mavis Hewitt may be scotched first thing in the morning, for all I know. So I'll have to get down to the usual routine of checking the local disappearances.'

'I hope, for your sake, that the laboratory can narrow down the time range for you,' said the colonel. 'You'll have the devil of a job as it is, in following up all the missing persons for even a ten-year period.'

There was a tap at the door. A constable from the charge room downstairs brought in a large envelope and laid it on the desk in front of the colonel.

'A patrol car has just brought this from Aber, sir,' he said, before saluting and marching out. Again Pacey had a slight military hallucination.

'It's addressed to you, Superintendent,' said Barton. He waited intently while the detective tore the package open to take out a folded newspaper and a sheet of paper.

'From Sergeant Evans – he's on the ball all right.' Pacey read from the note. 'He says he met the editor of the *Cardigan Voice* on the street just after I'd left, and asked him to open up the office. He got the copy of the paper for the week after the date on the police report and has sent it down. It saves us a few hours.'

'I hope the sergeant didn't let on to the man what it was all about,' fretted the colonel, holding his hand out for the note.

'No, Evans is all there, sir. He knows the ropes all right.' Pacey offered the newspaper to the colonel, but Barton waved it back.

'No, no, Pacey. This is your affair. You read it first.'

Willie Rees, sitting silently watching the play, knew that this was another bit of the chief's gamesmanship.

The paper, which had probably been lying untouched for the last thirty-three years, was slightly yellow and brittle, but otherwise perfect.

The style of the layout and printing was strange to Pacey's eyes as he opened the pages; and the quality of the photographs was poor by modern standards.

One of these pictures on an inside page caught his eye.

'Here it is; a photo of her – that's damn useful. There's a short column below it about her, too.'

'Read it out, there's a good chap,' asked the colonel, fairly bristling with interest now.

Pacey folded the paper across his knee and recited the passage for the benefit of the others.

'"Tremabon farmer's wife missing. Sister asks for help in tracing woman ... Mrs Jessie Randall of Liverpool, is anxious to discover the whereabouts of her sister, Mrs Mavis Hewitt, pictured above."

"Mrs Randall told our reporter that she had not heard from her sister for almost two months and, on coming to the district today to make inquiries, had been told by neighbours that Mrs Hewitt had not been seen for some weeks. When our reporter visited her home at Bryn Glas Farm, Tremabon, he was told by her husband, Mr Roland Hewitt that his wife had gone away and that he refused to discuss the matter."

"Mrs Randall has sought the aid of the police. Anyone having any information as to the whereabouts of the lady is asked to contact either their local police station or the editor of this paper.".'

Pacey stopped reading but did not raise his eyes from the paper.

'Is that all it says, Superintendent?' Barton asked impatiently.

Pacey gave a low whistle.

'No, there's a bit more. A very interesting bit, too. "The missing woman is twenty-six years of age, of slight build, about five foot four inches in height, with a fresh complexion and auburn hair. When last seen she was wearing a green linen suit with black shoes and hat.".'

Pacey laid the paper carefully on the desk.

'Twenty-six, five foot four and auburn hair,' he repeated, smoothing the newspaper with a big hand. 'We're getting warm, sir, aren't we?'

Chapter Seven

Things moved quickly on the following morning, the Tuesday after the bones were discovered.

Overnight, a message had arrived from Liverpool by telex, informing the Cardigan police that a Mrs Jessie Randall, late of 14 Speke Street, was alive and living nearby, at 24 Glebe Terrace.

'You'd better get up there straight away, Willie,' ordered Pacey. 'Take some of those pictures of the jewellery with you. You might strike lucky with something.'

The first albums of photographs had been delivered already – thanks to some overtime put in by the detective-constable who had taken them – and Rees left in a car for Liverpool with a bundle of pictures to show to the sister.

Pacey skipped through some other work in his office, then collected Detective Sergeant Mostyn from the CID office next to his own room.

'We're going up to Tremabon to use the rubber hosepipes on a few of those characters in the village,' he said cheerfully as they made their way down to his car. 'It's about time some of these bloody scandalmongers were sorted out. They get on my wick, the nasty old devils. But I must admit that they seem to have found something juicy to gnash their gums on this time.'

Mostyn was an aloof young man, only condescending to speak when he had something important to say.

Charles Pacey, with his gruff good humour, was a bit suspicious of the sergeant's manner; but he recognized the ability and good record of the younger man. Pacey was also doubtful of the sergeant's dandyish clothes, waved hair and dapper, fair moustache. Only the previous week, he had growled to Willie Rees, 'I never know what to make of these blokes who wear suede shoes and use aftershave lotion.'

On the trip to Tremabon, Mostyn was a little more talkative than usual – perhaps to offset the shock which Pacey had experienced in seeing him wearing a short camel-hair coat and American-style felt hat.

He listened carefully to Pacey's account of the case so far and showed the superintendent that he had already a good grasp of the affair by making some sensible comments.

'I wonder if Hewitt knows that we're interested in him. No chance of him skipping, I suppose.'

Pacey, looking like an unemployed labourer alongside his immaculate sergeant, wrinkled up his fat nose.

'I should think he's got wind of the local gossip by now – it's impossible not to in a small place like Tremabon. But, even assuming that he does know something about his wife's disappearance, I'm sure he wouldn't bolt. That would cook his goose straight away. And he doesn't know how much we know, does he?'

Mostyn didn't consider this bit of rhetoric worth an answer and stared out of the window at the rain-soaked hedges flashing past. 'Odd that his nephew should be in at the finding of these flaming bones.'

Pacey spoke reflectively – not expecting, nor getting, an answer from the sergeant. 'Nothing sinister in it, I know – seems a nice young chap. I'm sorry that he might have a bit of a shock coming his way.'

The logic of this pricked Mostyn into speech.

'From what you've told me, Super, you're going to need a devil of a lot of corroboration before you can slap anything on this man Hewitt.'

Pacey laughed shortly.

'There's a world of difference between charging a man and asking him questions, sonny. I'm going to start rubbing his nose in it as soon as we see him. You may know all the bookwork, lad, but you've still got a lot to learn. Grind 'em down fine in the beginning, that's the secret. If they've got nothing to hide, then no harm's done. But, if they have, either fright or anger will shake it out of 'em. Hammer them right from the start, that's the thing to do!'

Mostyn shot him a sideways glance containing all the finer shades of disapproval and disdain, but he said nothing.

Pacey was driving the police Austin himself and was blithely ignoring the few speed limits between Cardigan and their destination. They arrived at Tremabon at ten o'clock and Pacey inquired at once for the location of Roland Hewitt's cottage.

'We'll go and see the old boy first,' he said, swinging the car into the narrow lane that led up to the house. 'Then we can come back later, if need be, and rattle him again.'

As they reached the yard in front of the blue cottage, the old man appeared from the barn with two empty buckets. He stood as if frozen, gazing at the black car with the prominent 'Police' sign on the radiator.

Pacey stopped the car and walked with Mostyn across the cobbles towards Roland, who still stood petrified.

'Would you happen to be Mr Hewitt – Mr Roland Hewitt?' Pacey's voice was flat, neither pleasant, nor menacing.

No sign of the rubber truncheon yet, Mostyn thought cynically.

The old man came to life again and the buckets swung gently as he said that he was Roland Hewitt.

'We're police officers,' explained Pacey.

'Aye, I didn't think you were firemen,' said Roland dryly, swinging a bucket in the direction of the radiator sign. His face looked grey to Mostyn, but he seemed quite in control of himself. Pacey, with his many years' experience of interrogation, sensed that the old man was half-afraid, half-defiant.

'I'd like to ask you a few questions, Mr Hewitt,' said Pacey.

Roland sighed and dropped his buckets with a clatter.

'I thought you would, sooner or later. Come on in.' He slouched in front of them towards the front door, back bent, his whole attitude one of resigned apathy.

'All right, Twm.' He patted the dog who growled suspiciously at the two men who followed him into the kitchen.

Roland shuffled to his chair at the hearth and waved them to two others, opposite.

He looked older than Pacey had expected. He saw a lean, leathery caricature of a man, his cropped white hair bristling incongruously above his watery pale eyes. His sunken cheeks framed a sad mouth and Pacey felt that here was a man patiently waiting for a sad life to drag to its close. The detective almost ashamedly found that he already felt sorry for the man he had come to browbeat, even before he had asked a single question.

'I've got an idea that you already know why we've called,' he began quietly. 'By the way, I'm Superintendent Pacey and this is Sergeant Mostyn.'

Roland avoided his gaze and stared into the grate.

'Ay, those busybodies down in the village set you on to me, no doubt.'

'Your nephew, Mr Adams, isn't at home, then?'

'No, he's down with his young lady – Miss Ellis-Morgan.'

Pacey was strangely thankful for that. He liked Peter and now, almost against his will, he found himself sorry for his uncle. He began his questioning by jumping in with both feet.

'Mr Hewitt – I'd like you to tell me what happened to your wife in nineteen twenty-nine.'

Roland began rocking backwards and forwards on his seat, hands clasped on his lap.

'You know as much as I do, mister.'

'I don't think so, Mr Hewitt. Come on now, let's hear your version of it.'

'She just went out from the farm one day and never came back – that's the whole story, you can take it or leave it.' Roland's voice held a quavering defiance.

'I see. She just walked out and "never came back".' Pacey sounded professionally disbelieving. 'And what about all these fights and quarrels I've been hearing about, eh?' Pacey omitted to mention that, so far, all he'd heard was third-hand rumour from the village constable.

Roland glared at him. 'You've been listening to that damn man down in the Lamb and Flag. He's the one who caused most of this trouble, that Ceri Lloyd – carrying on with her and encouraging her in her badness.'

'So you admit that you were on bad terms with your wife?'

Roland peered over his glasses. His agitation seemed to have given way to suspicion for the moment.

'Of course I do – I've admitted it before, haven't I? You should know. You've got all the papers and forms I had to sign all them years ago. It was you police and those damn reporters that drove me away from here in the first place.'

He paused and looked keenly at the detectives, first at Pacey and then at the silent Mostyn.

'What's the idea of pestering me all over again, eh? You don't seem to know much about the affair. If you think I've got anything to do with that body up on the cliff, as you obviously do think, then you can go away and stop bothering me right now. Having a few words and a slap with a wife is one thing, but doing away with her is quite another.'

Charles Pacey felt that the interview was suddenly going all wrong. The old man's manner had changed from one of helpless resignation to defiant aggression in a few moments. He decided to turn the heat on a bit more.

'Wait a bit. Wait a bit,' he said gruffly. 'I'm asking the questions. Listen now, your wife was twenty-six when she "left" you, wasn't she?' He managed to turn the 'left' into a sneer of disbelief. Mostyn decided that this must be the start of the grinding-down process.

'Aye, you know that as well as I do – or should,' muttered the old man.

'Never mind what I know, or don't know. Just answer the questions. Now then, she had red hair, didn't she?'

Hewitt nodded sullenly.

Pacey swung round to Mostyn. 'Hear that, Sergeant – twenty-six and red hair!'

Mostyn had no idea what he was supposed to reply to that, so he kept quiet.

Pacey's head whipped back to Roland. 'And she was five foot four, wasn't she?' he snapped.

These tactics were beginning to strike home at the old man. He looked anxiously from one to the other.

'Well, was she?'

'Yes, I dare say you know she was,' he said haltingly.

'And she "just walked out" one day and "never came back"?' Pacey turned the words into the ultimate in sarcasm.

Roland made no answer. These obtuse references to Mavis's age, hair and height had frightened him.

'Have you got anything else to tell us, Hewitt?' Pacey dropped the 'Mr' at this point.

Roland's voice came in a whisper.

'No, I haven't. My conscience is clear. Whatever you know, or think you know. I've got nothing to be afraid of, nor nothing to hide.'

'Well, where did she go, eh?'

'I don't know. Why should I know, if her sister didn't?'

'Why indeed. What date did she disappear?'

'I … I can't remember. It was a long time ago.'

'Did she take any clothes with her?'

'I don't know. I mean, yes, I'm sure she did. She always took a bag when she went away.'

'A bag, eh? Wouldn't float long, with a few stones inside, would it?'

'I don't know what you mean,' croaked Roland.

'Did you have a fight the day she left you?'

'No more than usual.'

'No more than usual! Did you fight every day?'

The old man's eyes flickered behind the thick glasses. 'Most times, towards the end.'

'Towards what end, Mr Hewitt.' The 'Mr' came back in a sickly, sinister form.

'When she went, of course.'

'Why did she go, the last time?'

'I'm trying to tell you, I don't know.' Roland's reedy voice was high with panic. 'You got no right to come badgering an old man like this. I don't know any more now than when I talked to police all them years ago.'

'Where did she go – did she say?' Pacey pursued relentlessly.

'For God's sake, man, if I knew, we wouldn't be wondering where she was, would we? I don't know, I tell you – I don't know!'

'But she didn't go to Liverpool, did she?'

'She might have gone to China, for all I knew or cared. But her sister came here looking for her, so she couldn't have gone there.'

'So where do you think she went?'

'I don't know!' Roland almost screamed this.

Pacey kept the questions going fast and furious.

'You admit hitting and bruising her?'

'I already have – years ago. She came at me with a knife, not long before.'

'Oh, are you trying to say now, that you did something to her in self-defence?'

'I'm not saying anything – all I did was to hit her about half as much as she hit me. Then she went away and never came back. Can't you leave me alone?'

'You allege that she tried to kill you?'

'I didn't say that – it was just her temper – a terrible one she had!'

'It wasn't you that tried to attack her, and she defended herself, was it?'

Roland looked shocked. His spiky hair stood up on end and his restless eyes roved like those of a cornered animal.

Charlie has got him on the run, thought the sergeant, *but he's too short of facts to catch the old boy out yet*.

The same thought must have occurred to Pacey; for, after a few more aggressive lunges at Hewitt, which achieved nothing apart from increasing the old man's terror, the detective suddenly got up and wagged his head at Mostyn.

'Come on, Sergeant. I think we'll give Mr Hewitt some time to think. Perhaps he'll decide to help us more than he has so far. We'll be back, Mr Hewitt. We'll see ourselves out.'

They left the old farmer sitting and shaking with apprehension. As they crossed the yard, followed by a growling sheepdog, Pacey spoke to his colleague.

'I had to give it a try. But either the old fellow is a real cunning bastard, or he really doesn't know a thing about what happened to his missus.'

Mostyn showed a streak of compassion that Pacey hadn't suspected.

'I felt sorry for the old man – he seems harmless enough. You hammering him like that has probably taken years off his life.'

'No, if he's lily white, it'll soon be forgotten. And, if he isn't, he deserves what's coming. Let's go and see this chap in the pub, the fat bloke everyone talks about.'

A few minutes' drive brought them to the whitewashed porch of the Lamb and Flag. It was well before opening time – though, as Pacey knew only too well, this made little difference to the sales in the average Welsh public house. He got out of the car and hammered on the closed outer door with a fist. When it was opened, Pacey was confronted by the fattest man he had ever seen.

Ceri Lloyd had evidently just got out of bed. Wearing a crumpled and collarless shirt, he was in the act of hooking his braces over his vast chest as he squinted blearily through the half-open door. His piggy eyes stared out of an unshaven face at his visitors.

'I'm Detective Superintendent Pacey – and this is Sergeant Mostyn. I'd like a few words with you please.'

Ceri's morning lethargy left him in an instant. A grin split his great cheeks and he bobbed his head rapidly.

'Ah, yes, I thought you'd be around. Come on in.'

He stood aside and Pacey, himself a small giant, pushed past him into the stone-flagged public bar.

Looking around at the chairs piled on the tables, the cloth over the beer pumps, and smelling the sour aroma of stale drink, he thought what a miserable place a public house was, out of licensing hours.

Lloyd pulled down a couple of chairs and set them near to the counter. He waved at the array of bottles on the bar shelves.

'Can I offer you anything, gentlemen?' he said anxiously, dry-washing his hands as he spoke.

Pacey declined abruptly. He had taken an instant dislike to the great waxy-faced landlord and wanted to get his business with him over as quickly as he could.

'How old are you, Lloyd?' he began.

This put Ceri right out of his stride. He was all set to

launch out on a tidal wave of malicious gossip about Roland Hewitt, and actually had his flabby mouth open ready to go, when Pacey stopped him in his tracks with this strange question. His lips shut again and he groped for another chair for himself.

'How old? Er, let's see, I'm sixty-one, yes. Born nineteen oh one. Why?'

'And you've lived in Tremabon all your life?'

'Er … yes.'

'So you might be in a position to remember a Mrs Mavis Hewitt?'

Lloyd's face cracked open again into a leer.

'Ah, Superintendent, you're playing with me. Of course, I do.'

Pacey was not amused. 'You mean you *do* remember her?'

The publican wagged a finger roguishly. 'I'll say I do. You won't find anyone in the village, alive or dead, who knew her better. And that goes for the old fool she married, as well. He never knew the first thing about her, really.'

Pacey slouched in his chair, hands thrust deeply into the pockets of his raincoat.

'You were, shall we say, on "intimate terms" with her, then?'

Ceri actually winked this time.

'You can say that, sir – intimate in more ways than one.' Little dribbles of saliva appeared at the corners of his drooping lips. Pacey had a strong urge to kick his great fat backside.

'How long did you know her, before she vanished from Tremabon?'

Lloyd considered this for a moment. 'I'd say about four years, all told. She came as a maid' – he leered again as he said the word – 'as a maid to one of the big houses around here. Then she married Hewitt about eighteen months –

no, two years – after that. It was about another two years before he did away with the poor girl – so that makes it about four years all told that I knew her.'

The superintendent scowled.

'Why are you so definite that her husband had anything to do with her disappearance? You can say what you like to me, but I'd advise you to go easy on your tongue anywhere else.'

Ceri smiled deprecatingly. 'Of course not, officer. I'm not one for spreading scandal, you know. But everyone knows that Hewitt had something to do with her going so sudden, like she did.'

'You'd better tell me all you know about the whole business.'

'Well, Mavis used to come down here to see me a lot. I've never married, see,' he added with almost a simper. 'Towards the end, she was getting more and more desperate. I think she would have left the old swine soon, if he hadn't done for her first.'

'What makes you say that?'

'She sometimes asked questions of me about getting a divorce, and about separation and all that. Anyway, they were having real bad fights. They done that most of the time they were married, but they got a sight worse towards the end.'

'How do you know that?'

'She showed me her bruises more than once. On the arms and neck, and other places.'

'Did you know that she used to go away a lot – sometimes for weeks at a time?'

'Lord, of course I did! She was quite a girl, was Mavis. Brought up in the town and fond of a bit of life. She used to go home to Liverpool and stay with her sister. I know she had plenty of men friends up there.'

'Why should you think that she was dead? She had been away plenty of times before – and you've just said

85

yourself that she was talking about leaving her husband.'

Lloyd shrugged his shoulders in a gargantuan heave. 'She would have said something to me about it. She always told me when she was going away, even if she didn't tell her old man. And, anyway, she didn't come back, did she? And no one has seen a clip of her since.'

Pacey couldn't fault the logic of this, so turned to something else.

'How old would this sister be?'

'About three or four years older than Mavis, I'd say. She must have been about thirty when she came looking for her.'

Mostyn beat Pacey to the calculation. 'That'll make her about sixty-three now.'

The superintendent glowered at him. 'All right; I can count. Now, Lloyd, let's have it straight. Do all your winks and nods mean that Mavis Hewitt was your mistress – both before and after she was married?'

Ceri seemed to be not in the least embarrassed.

'Yes, that's about it, officer. I wasn't so plump in those days, and only being a year or two older than her – not ten more, like Roland Hewitt – well, we seemed to hit it off well together.'

'Did Hewitt know about this at the time?'

'I dunno. He must have been mighty daft if he didn't, 'cause all the rest of the village did. Still, he never spoke to me, nor even came near me, so I didn't have much chance to tell.'

'You're saying, then, that there was never any bad feeling between the two of you?'

'There might 'a been on his side, but it didn't matter a tinker's cuss to me. It was his wife I was interested in, not 'im. And, if he wasn't man enough to hold her himself, then I didn't see why I shouldn't have the benefit myself.'

Again Pacey's foot itched to come into violent contact with Lloyd's trouser seat.

'Let's get to some details of the girl. You seem in as good a position as any to give them,' he said shrewishly. 'What did she actually look like?'

Ceri gazed thoughtfully at the back of his hand.

'Pretty, she was. Real pretty. Middling size – perhaps five foot three or so. Lovely figure by damn, it was!'

'What about eyes and hair?'

'Oh, red hair. Natural red, not dyed like these days. It was a dark, sort of coppery colour.'

'And eyes?' prompted the detective.

Lloyd looked doubtful. 'Damn, do you know, I couldn't swear to them. Not brown nor blue, but any colour from grey to green. Difficult to describe, if you know what I mean.'

Pacey, thinking of the brown bones and sickening legs, said gruffly, 'It doesn't matter. Did she have any physical deformities, or marks? Perhaps you noticed some that *other* people wouldn't see.'

The sarcasm was lost on Ceri who wrinkled his pasty brow in thought.

'Certainly no deformities,' he said in a slightly shocked voice. 'She had a lovely body on her. Had a few moles and marks, but nothing I could describe exactly.'

'No diseases that you know of? Any operations or things like that?'

Ceri shook his head emphatically. 'No, she was perfect.'

'Any fractures, or arthritis?' Pacey was scraping the bottom of the barrel now.

Ceri again denied any faults in his mistress's skeleton.

'Do you remember any jewellery she used to wear?'

'It's a long time ago, sir, thirty-odd years.'

'What about rings?'

'She sometimes had a wedding ring on.'

'What do you mean "sometimes"?'

Ceri leered revoltingly. 'She took it off when she was

on her way to Liverpool – used to cramp her style, I expect.'

'What sort was it?'

'I can't remember. Nothing special about it, I do know. The sort that you wouldn't notice unless it wasn't there, if you get me. Old Roland wouldn't be the one to go spending fancy money on a ring.'

'Can you remember anything about her clothes?'

'She was a smart dresser – for these parts, anyway. I don't know where she got the money to do it – or perhaps I can guess, come to think of it. Fancy clothes, they were. The old cats in the village used to call her all the names under the sun for being fast and a hussy. Hated the sight of her, most of them. They were all afraid that their husbands would go after her – and most of them would have, given the chance. She used to give anything in trousers the eye, just for the hell of it. Jealous as blazes, the Tremabon women were. If old Roland hadn't done her in, I wouldn't put it past one of them seeing her off!'

'She doesn't sound the sort that would marry Hewitt,' observed Pacey.

'No. Miles apart, they were. He was just a way of getting out of gentleman's service to her. A fair packet of money and a freehold farm he had, see. She regretted it pretty soon, though, for he was a tight-fisted old shark.'

Pacey was getting impatient. 'What was she wearing when you last saw her?'

Ceri spread his hands out in appeal. 'Damn it, Superintendent, I wouldn't notice a woman's clothes thirty minutes later, let alone thirty years!' He scratched his head. 'No, I don't know what she wore. All I know is she always looked smart.'

After a few more minutes, Pacey realized that the gross landlord had nothing more to offer in the way of information, apart from sheer speculation and rumour.

They left him standing on the doorstep, still fumbling

with his braces and trouser buttons, and drove off towards Aberystwyth.

'I'm going to get some information that's not so ruddy biased as that last lot,' said Pacey to Mostyn. 'Before we come back to tackle any more of these old codgers in the village, I'll try and find someone from the police who remembers the affair – and hope that the file from Records turns up, though I doubt it now.'

Mostyn became more communicative as they drove on.

'What a monstrous great belly that Lloyd chap had – looked like a wax Buddha that had been left too near to the fire.'

Pacey chuckled at the description. 'That just about sizes him up, lad. If he and Hewitt were the only attractions in the village for a smart girl like Mavis – well, all the other men must have been cross-eyed dwarves!'

'Will any of this second-hand evidence be any good in identifying the body?'

'No, damn all. Not in saying whether the body was Mavis, anyway. But, if the doctor and "lab" people can convince me it was her, it's the village gossip about the quarrels that will nail a charge on Hewitt. If we ever get that far, that is.'

Mostyn thought for a mile or so of the wet, winding road.

'As I see it, if the body definitely can be shown to be Mavis, then old Hewitt is for it. There can't be any other suspect, can there?'

Pacey shrugged. 'Unless her spurned lover, or a jealous wife, knocked her off. But how the hell we prove anything at all after thirty-odd years is beyond me. The standard of proof may come up to what the coroner needs, but I can never see an assize jury convicting Hewitt, even if the science boys satisfy everyone that the bones belong to Mavis. And they've got a long way to go to do that yet.'

While the two detectives were driving away from the Lamb and Flag, Peter Adams had arrived back at his uncle's cottage.

This time, he had heard plenty of rumours while he was out. Mary had poured out her version of the gossip as soon as he had arrived, having collected it from her daily help before breakfast. Although she was scornful of the whole affair, Peter could tell that she was worried about Roland. Typically, she was not anxious for herself, because she was engaged to his nephew; but she was disturbed about the old man's own peace of mind and the effect it might have on him. Peter did his best to laugh it off and to reassure her, but she remained anxious and preoccupied all the time he was there.

'What about the *Morning News* now,' she fretted. 'You can't possibly send any more copy to them.'

It had already struck Peter that he could hardly report the rumours that the remains might belong to the victim of his own uncle's violence. 'It's going to be difficult to get out of,' he replied. 'If I tell the editor that I can't carry on because my family might be involved, he'll have another chap down here like greased lightning. If I stop writing anything myself and the police give a statement to the other papers, I'll probably get fired.'

'Well, sweet, if the story has to come out, there's no point in blocking your own paper – but it's a difficult position, I'll admit.'

Eventually, he rang his office in Cardiff and spun a rather weak story about the police not wanting him to publish anything more, as he had been personally involved at the original finding of the remains. The sub-editor grudgingly accepted this and promised to send another man from Pembroke to see if the police had any further statements to make.

'You'd better get back to your uncle, Peter,' worried Mary later in the morning. 'The police are sure to go there

90

sooner or later, and it would be better if you were there as well when they come pestering old Roland.'

'A hell of a fine holiday this is going to be,' he said despondently as he kissed her goodbye and left Carmel House. He called in a couple of shops on the way home to buy bread and some cigarettes. In the first, he received some odd looks, but none of the usual small talk. In the little tobacconist's, kept by a cheerful widow, he had a flood of sympathetic chatter, the gist of it being that it was a pity that the old folks hadn't something better to do than make mountains out of a few silly molehills.

Peter returned to the cottage in an uneasy mood, which was justified as soon as he entered the kitchen. The table still carried the breakfast dishes and his uncle sat immobile in his chair by the unlit fire. He gave no greeting as Peter came in, but slowly raised his head as his nephew came across to stand over him.

'They've been already, boy.'

Peter stared down at Roland. 'Who have been?'

'The police, boy – just after you left.'

Peter dropped down into a chair facing the old man. 'They seem to know a lot about Mavis already – as good as gave me the tip they know this skeleton is hers.'

Roland's voice sounded flat and resigned. Peter tried to reassure him as he had tried with Mary.

'Look, they're asking questions all around the village about anyone who went missing about that time. Naturally, they'll come to ask you, as you were her husband. It doesn't mean to say that they think you had anything to do with her vanishing.'

Roland ran a hand through his bristly hair.

'They as good as told me it was her, boy. Same height. Same age. She had red hair, as well.'

Peter was shaken by this, but he tried to cover up his concern. He'd had no idea that the police had discovered that there was that much similarity between Mavis and the remains.

'Nonsense, they were trying the old gag of trying to make you say something incriminating by pretending that they knew it all already,' he said. 'That old Pacey is trying on a bit of his detective "gamesmanship". He wants to confuse and frighten you into saying something to incriminate yourself. But, as you've done nothing, he can't succeed, can he?'

Although unbeknown to Peter, he was fairly near to the truth, he felt none of the confidence that he tried to put into his words for Roland's sake.

'What's going to happen next, boy? I'm worried sick. All the gossip. And now these questions and the proof they say they've got. What's going to happen to me?'

His voice rose and cracked in a sudden spasm of hysteria. Peter jumped up and laid a comforting hand on the old man's shoulder.

'Now look, take it easy. I'll put some tea on and we'll talk this over, quietly and sensibly. We both know that you had nothing to do with anybody's death, so nothing at all can happen to you – nothing!'

Roland sat trembling, his bony hands clenching and unclenching.

'But what if it *is* Mavis? ... I don't know where she went that last day. It *might* be her, for all I know.'

Peter raised a hand.

'All right. All right. Say it is Mavis. I don't think the police could prove it in a month of Sundays. But if it is – all right! It's still nothing to do with you. You didn't kill her, so you've got nothing to be afraid of.' The old man muttered something that his nephew didn't catch. Peter filled a kettle and put it over the flame of a bottled gas stove in a corner of the kitchen.

Roland pulled himself together and shuffled over to get some cups and saucers together.

'They scared me, boy,' he said in a more normal tone.

'Coming here like that, frightened me, they have. What had I better do? I've got a solicitor over in Aber, the chap that did the deeds of this house. Should I call and see him?'

Peter shook his head. 'No need, not yet anyway, until the police start bothering you a lot more seriously. They're not accusing you openly of anything yet, and I don't suppose they ever will. They know no more than all those gossips in the village. By this time tomorrow, I don't mind betting that Pacey and his crowd will have found that the bones couldn't possibly have belonged to Aunt Mavis. It'll all die down and life will go back to being what it was before.'

Roland made the tea and slumped back into his chair, hands clasped around his warm cup.

'But what happened to her, boy, what happened to Mavis? She was attractive and bold. She could have been attacked and killed around here and hidden in the mine – but who would do a thing like that? Yet if it isn't her body, who else could it be? I've churned it over in my mind so much that I sometimes think that it could have been me that did it and never remembered nothing about it!'

Peter glared sternly at his uncle. 'For goodness' sake, don't talk that sort of rubbish! That's the kind of thing that will get you into trouble.'

Roland began rocking in his chair again, a sure sign of his agitation.

'But who else can it be, boy, who else?'

Peter was stumped for an answer and Roland pressed home his point. 'They must know how long the thing has been there, near enough, or they wouldn't have come bothering me. And no one – no one at all – disappeared from Tremabon in all the time I can remember, except Mavis. And if it is her, did I put her there? … *did* I do it, boy?'

Chapter Eight

While Peter and his uncle sat worrying, Pacey was again turning the archives of Aberystwyth police station upside down and Willie Rees was on his way to Liverpool. Another part of the drama was being played out in the serene buildings of the University at Swansea.

In a large first floor room, overlooking the park and the sweep of the bay, the furniture had been pushed back to the wall. Two senior members of the medical school staff squatted on the floor, like boys with a toy train set.

Instead of miniature rails and trucks, they had a white sheet spread on the parquet floor. This was covered with a bizarre jigsaw of bones.

Leighton Powell watched his companion put a small piece into position. 'That's the last one, Tom. How does it look from up there, Inspector Meadows?'

The police officer from the Forensic Science laboratory stood against a bench near the window. He was watching the antics of the two on the floor with obvious interest.

'Pretty good, sir. I'd say it looks as near to complete now as makes no difference. Do you want it photographed now, or are you going to do any more to it?'

Dr Tom Mitchell, the anatomist, whose room this was, climbed to his feet and stood looking critically at his handiwork.

'I'll have to shuffle them about a bit first, to allow for the cartilage of the joint spaces. That should give us the exact height then. What do you think of it, Leighton?'

The bald-headed forensic expert hauled himself off the floor and dusted down the knees of his suit as he looked at the grinning skull and loosely arranged bones on the sheet. As Meadows had said, the skeleton looked perfectly complete, the only odd feature being the thick, waxy flesh on the legs.

'Yes, it looks OK,' he replied. 'We may as well check our fancy calculations of the height by a direct measurement, I suppose.'

The tall, thin anatomist began arranging the bones with minute precision. He separated the rusty brown pieces one by one, starting at the neck, where the spinal bones joined the skull. The genial professor explained to Meadows what Mitchell was doing.

'The idea is to allow for the thickness of the gristle between the vertebrae of the spine and the cartilage in the knee and hip joints. We've already calculated what her height should be during life, by applying special formulae to individual bones, especially in the leg. But it would be nice to check the answer by putting the bones in their "living" position and then running a tape measure over the whole lot.'

'Wouldn't that be the best way, in any case?' asked Meadows.

Leighton Powell pursed his lips. 'Not necessarily. It's difficult to get the bones to lie on a flat surface in the way they do in the body. The spine has three curves, more marked in women. You can't always reproduce that accurately with a heap of loose bones. But the main use of the calculation method is when only a part of the skeleton, or even only one bone, is available.'

Tom Mitchell straightened his own back for a moment and added his explanations. 'More often than not, there are bones missing all over the skeleton. We're unusually lucky with this one in having nearly all of it to play with. Years ago, some anatomists made accurate measurements of hundreds of bones and made up formulae for each one – so that, now, we can get an estimate of the owner's size from any limb bone.'

Powell nodded as Mitchell settled back to his jigsaw.

'Naturally, the more bones there are available, the more accurate we can be – by taking the average of a lot of calculations.'

Meadows looked curiously at the anatomist as he carefully spaced out each bone from its neighbour.

'I see – he's allowing for the soft tissue that's rotted away.'

'That's it. Each intervertebral disc – the things that "slip" in your back – is about a quarter of an inch thick. So he's spacing the bones that far apart.'

Mitchell came slowly upright again, holding his own back with one hand. 'I think I've dislocated one of mine in the process. I'm getting too old for this stooping game. It's worse than weeding the garden.'

'Let's have a go. You've done it all except the legs.'

The professor knelt on the edge of the sheet and finished off the lower limbs. He placed the long leg bones in position, including the one that the small boy had found.

The anatomy lecturer looked thoughtfully at the finished job for a moment, then nodded his approval.

'Right, Leighton, let's run the tape over her. Will you hold one end level with the top of the skull?'

They held a metal rule over the skeleton and read off the length.

'About five foot four, I make it,' said Mitchell. 'Dead on, eh? That's what the calculations said.'

Powell grinned, his pink face boyish in spite of his middle age and morbid profession. 'Be damned queer if it wasn't, Tom. Guessing the height of a complete body is as easy as stealing a blind man's stick.'

'I can get my photographer up now, can I?' asked Meadows. 'He should be down in the entrance with his stuff.'

The police photographer duly arrived, loaded down

with bags and a massive tripod. While the skeleton was being put on film, the other three went over to Mitchell's littered desk to look at some other photographs that Powell had brought with him.

'These were taken yesterday with a low-powered microscope,' he explained. 'They show the saw cuts on the arm bone in close-up.'

The glossy prints were passed between the men. They showed the surface of the humerus of the skeleton, with the area of attempted amputation greatly magnified.

'The main one goes about halfway through the bone,' explained Powell. 'And, just below it, there is a smaller slot which I presume was a false start before the main cut.'

Meadows studied the picture magnified the most.

'You can see the scratches from the saw teeth on the walls of the slot in this one,' he commented.

'Yes, they seem very close together,' agreed Mitchell.

'What about this false start – any special significance in that, Professor?' asked Meadows.

'No, I don't think so – just a failure to hold the saw in the first cut tightly enough. Once it slipped out, the soft tissues would obscure the hole and stop him putting the saw blade back in the same place.'

'The blade seems to be about a sixteenth of an inch wide – what sort of tool would that be, I wonder?'

Meadows looked at his own print closely. He felt more at home talking about saw blades than about bare bones.

'Yes, I noticed this on the bone itself,' he said. 'It could well be a hacksaw with fine teeth like this.'

Powell agreed with the inspector. 'I think that's very likely, though it's a bit thicker than the little hacksaws I'm accustomed to using.'

'You can get many different types, sir; we see them in our burglary cases. The type of cut depends on the number and spread of the teeth, as well as the thickness of the blade.'

The photographer finished taking his pictures and came across the room to ask if there were any more to be done.

Mitchell looked at the pathologist questioningly. 'What about the skull? Shall we have a couple of that for a go at superimposition, if the opportunity ever arises?'

Powell agreed again. 'We can have a picture of that hole in the skull and the teeth at the same time.'

'What about that hole, sir – any ideas on what it means?' asked Meadows.

Powell looked dubious. 'I'll never be able to get up in court and say that it was caused before death. It could just as easily have happened when the roof fell in on her.'

The pictures were taken and the photographer struggled away with his apparatus.

'That's about all I can do for you now, I think,' said Dr Mitchell. 'I'll pack this lady up in a box for you to take away.'

To save tedious rearrangement in the future, he slid the vertebrae onto a length of rubber gas-tubing and secured each end with a safety pin. The big bones he put in separate plastic bags; and the hands and feet also had a bag apiece.

After thanking the anatomist for his help, Powell and Meadows carried their trophies of the chase downstairs. They drove in Meadows' car across the college grounds to the pathology institute, which held the Department of Forensic Medicine.

Here, in Powell's room, they dumped the bones and concentrated on something else.

The professor unlocked a drawer in his desk and took out two small polythene envelopes.

'Here's some of the hair that was found,' he explained. 'This lot here is as it was found, and the other has been cleaned. I've had them in my possession all the time, just for the record of continuity of evidence. I'm handing them back to you now. All right? We don't want some smart alec of a defence counsel taking the mickey out of us if it ever gets to court – which God forbid!'

Meadows held up the two transparent packets to the window. He studied them with interest. The liaison officer was a careful man, whose long experience was made all the more valuable by a great deal of common sense and quiet enthusiasm for his job.

'There's certainly a marked difference in the colour of the two samples. What did you do to this one?' He held up the bag of cleaned hair.

'Just got rid of the years accumulation of mud and slime,' replied Powell. 'I washed them in an alcohol-ether mixture, and they came up like new – as the TV detergent adverts say! I've got a couple of strands mounted on a slide, if you'd like to see them.'

He went to a bench and switched on the lamp of a binocular microscope which stood there. He fiddled with the controls for a moment before beckoning to Meadows.

'There, have a look at that. A nice auburn colour, though you can see the true tint better in the hand. I always feel that the microscope makes hair look blonder than it really is.'

As with hacksaws, Meadows felt more at home with hairs than with bones. Fibres of all sorts were frequently sent to the forensic laboratory, being common clues after crimes of violence and robberies. He studied the golden-red strands for a moment.

'No doubt about this being human, I suppose?'

'Looks all right to me,' answered the professor. 'The size, cortex and scale pattern are all OK. One odd thing, though. There are no roots at all. Nor remains of hair bulbs.'

'What does that mean?'

'Every end that I've seen has been either a frayed or cut one. Many of the hairs are cut at both ends – so it looks as if the hair was severed from the scalp before burial.'

Meadows looked puzzled. 'That's more than a bit odd, eh?'

'I don't know. If the killer went so far as to try to cut an arm off, he might have thought of removing the hair as well, to make identification more difficult. Though why he should have put it back with the body is beyond me.'

'Is it cut at the scalp, do you think, or just anywhere?' Powell waved one of the plastic bags at Meadows.

'Some of this hair is a good eight inches long, so I'd think it was almost the full length. As far as I can remember, women used to have fairly short hair styles in the twenties and early thirties. Didn't they call it "bobbed" or something?'

'What about the roots in the scalp? Wouldn't they survive if the actual hair did?'

'Oh, it would be impossible to find the roots once the flesh of the scalp disintegrated. They would be a tiny fraction of an inch long and would vanish in all that muck and rubble around the body.'

Meadows collected the packets of hair and prepared to leave.

'So we're definitely looking for a red-haired woman, five foot four in height, between twenty-two and thirty years of age, sir?' He asked this as he was going through the door of the professor's room into the corridor.

Powell walked slowly with him to the lift. 'Yes, I think that's a fair description. As near as we can get it without being misleadingly accurate, anyway.'

'How can you be so definite about the age range, just from looking at the bones?'

'Well, a person grows by adding calcium compounds – chalky stuff – along a line of gristle, called the "epiphysis", which lies near the ends of the bones. When the bone reaches its maximum size and stops growing, this line vanishes. We call this the "fusion" time. Each particular bone in the body has its own set time for fusion, which is fairly constant, within a year or two. For example, the lower end of that bone the boy found would fuse at eighteen, give or take a year each way. The last ones to go are at about twenty-two to twenty-five years, usually the earlier age in women. We X-rayed all the bones in this case – that's the best way to see the epiphyses – and found that they had all fused, so that she must be at least twenty-two. In kids, we can tell the age almost exactly. But, as age increases, it gets harder and harder.'

Meadows was still full of curiosity. 'Why do you put the upper age at thirty?'

'That's a bit less definite, I admit. But, as a rule, the plates of bone forming the skullcap begin to fuse at about that age, starting on the inside first. There was no sign of this in "Flossie" here, so obviously she is less than thirty. Another thing is the fusion of the spheno-occipital joint.'

Meadows looked blankly at Powell and the doctor grinned.

'That's just a fancy name for one of the fusion lines in the floor of the skull. It seizes up at about twenty-five, and this girl's is just in the process of doing that.'

'So she's twenty-five,' suggested Meadows.

'Ah, these things are a bit chancy – a few years either way has to be allowed. It's the sum total of a lot of facts that adds up to the most probable age. She's got changes in other sutures in her skull, and in the front joint of her pelvis, which suggests that she is in the middle twenties. But, in all honesty, I can't be more definite than twenty-two to thirty.'

The pair halted outside the lift and the professor thumbed the call button for the policeman.

'I know you keep calling it "she", sir; is that a dead certainty, or another strong probability, like the age?'

Powell laughed. 'You're a regular doubting Thomas, Inspector. No, as far as the sex goes, I'll stick my neck out all the way. The chances of saying whether a collection of bones is male or female increases proportionately to the number of bones available for examination. When, as in this case, the whole skeleton is present, the chances reach a hundred per cent.'

'What's so different in the bones, then?'

'Oh, the general appearance to start with. The woman's are lighter and smoother; they haven't got the strong ridges where a man's bigger muscles are attached, for one thing. Then again, the pelvic bones are different; the female's are flatter and more open – connected with childbirth, I suppose. There are umpteen other differences, too. The eye sockets are square in the man, round in the woman. The pelvis is the main thing to go for, but all the bones have some sex difference.'

The lift appeared. Meadows, having had his fill of technicalities, left the pathologist to carry on with the day's bag of post-mortem examinations for the local coroner.

Chapter Nine

The police car crept slowly down the street like a great black beetle, the drizzle turning the windows into frosted glass. Detective Inspector Rees and a plain-clothes man from the Liverpool CID peered out through the rain, trying to glimpse the street numbers on the houses. Through the windscreen, rows of dismal terraced houses could be seen stretching ahead of them, dockside cranes rearing up beyond them and factory chimneys belching smoke in the distance.

'That was eighteen, driver,' called out the local constable, 'Here's twenty-two coming up – twenty-four – hold it!' The car stopped outside a house identical with hundreds of its neighbours. Number 24 Glebe Terrace. It had grimy green paint on the window frames, and the front door had been varnished in the long distant past. Rees opened the car door and jumped out into the rain.

'Will you want me?' asked the local detective, hopefully.

'No, thanks. This shouldn't take long,' replied Rees.

He slammed the door and ran for shelter to the porch which overhung the pavement, there being no front garden. He banged the cast-iron knocker vigorously.

The door was opened by a grey-haired woman wearing an apron over a drab dress. She was in her sixties, Rees estimated, which should be about right for Mavis's elder sister. She had a thickset, flabby body and a massive pair of legs. Her feet were squeezed into a down-at-heel pair of bedroom slippers.

A miserable face, with deep furrows and pouchy eyes,

glared at him across the threshold.

'Mrs Randall?' he asked, and got a curt nod in reply.

'I'm a police officer, Detective Inspector Rees, from …'

She cut him short. 'You're the chap from Wales, I suppose. They told me yesterday that you'd be coming.' She stood aside and grudgingly motioned him to come into the passage.

'You'd better come in, I suppose. In there.' She pointed to the door of the parlour facing the street.

Rees went in and stood in the centre of the worn carpet. The room was full of unused furniture and ugly knick-knacks. It smelt strongly of damp.

'Took you long enough to get here, didn't it?' growled Jessie Randall, following him in.

Rees stared at her in surprise. 'Long enough? We only had the message last night, and I've come straight up here this morning.'

Her lacklustre eyes stared stonily at him.

'It took you over thirty years to get here, to my way of thinking,' she said sarcastically. 'What's the use of raking all the past up now? It was then that the old devil should have been caught.'

Willie Rees sighed to himself. He could see that this interview was going to be an uphill struggle.

'Well, we don't know yet that this body does belong to your sister, Mrs Randall. That's one reason why I've come to see you. Your evidence may be the most important of the lot in deciding whether this is Mavis Hewitt.' He had tried this appeal to her vanity as a lubricant to the questioning process. Her expression remained as unfriendly as ever.

'You'd better sit down,' was all she said. Rees perched himself on the edge of a creaking armchair and the woman lowered herself onto a piano stool near the door.

'What d'you want to know about my poor sister?'

'When was the last time you saw her alive?' asked Rees. He produced a few sheets of paper and laid them on the packet of photographs that he took from his raincoat pocket.

The woman's pouchy eyes looked steadily at him.

'I can't give you exact dates, but it was about six weeks before I had the first of the letters.'

This was news to Rees. 'What letters are these?'

Jessie Randall looked at him with impatience.

'Don't you coppers know anything? It's all in the statement I made at the time.'

Rees avoided telling her that the file of the case had vanished as completely as had Mavis Hewitt herself.

He tried to 'soft-soap' her again. 'Yes, but I'd like to hear about it again from you yourself. There's nothing like going back to the actual witness for the best account. It's better than reading all the second-hand stories we get.'

She sniffed at the dubious compliment and began to speak of the events of the late nineteen twenties.

'Mavis came up to stay with me about the June or July of that year – twenty-nine, that would be, of course. I had a few letters, as usual, after she went back – she used to write about every fortnight. The last two letters were the ones I kept, as they had the bits in them about old Hewitt. Then the letters stopped, and I never saw her again.'

Willie was horrified to see the wrinkled face suddenly crack into a sob. She hauled a grubby handkerchief from the pocket of her even grubbier apron and dabbed it around her eyes. He hurried on with his questions.

'What did these particular letters say?'

The tears vanished as quickly as they had come, and her face took up its old sour look once more.

'You'd know if you took the trouble to read what I said to the police all them years ago. They said how she was being ill-treated by that swine of a husband of hers. My poor little girl, she had a terrible time with him. It isn't right that he should have got away with it for all these years. What's the use of punishing him now, an old man like he is?'

For the first time, her voice showed some animation and lifted out of its usual dull monotone.

'Have you still got these letters, Mrs Randall?'

'Perhaps I have; perhaps I haven't,' she said unhelpfully.

'We'd very much like to see them, if you could manage to find them,' Rees almost pleaded.

'I'll have a look presently,' she conceded, with another loud sniff.

'What was the next thing after the letters?'

'Nothing – that was the trouble,' she snapped. 'I didn't get my usual regular letters after these two. I wrote a couple of times myself, but there was no reply. In the end, I went down to the damned place to see what was going on.'

'What did you think *might* have been going on?'

'I don't know. It struck me that Roland Hewitt was either stopping her from writing, or tearing up my letters before Mavis got them. He always hated me, did that man. He knew that I could see him for what he really was. A scandal, him marrying a bit of a thing like her. I did my best to stop it, but Mavis was too headstrong, as usual. Him ten years or more older than her – disgusting, I called it. And he was as mean and nasty as they make them.'

'So you didn't get on with Mr Hewitt?'

'Get on with him! I hated the sight of him. I always did, even before he started injuring my poor sister – poor little Mavis.'

For another awful moment, Willie thought she was going to dissolve into tears again at the memory of her obviously hard-boiled sister; but, after a brief quiver, her mouth hardened again.

'Jealous, that was his trouble. He wanted to hold her for

himself; he wasn't willing for her to have any life of her own. I know she was a bit of a little madam sometimes, but she always went back to him, poor thing. That summer, though, things came to head down there.'

'What makes you so sure that he *did* do anything violent to her?'

Mrs Randall looked scornfully at the detective.

'Well, where is she now, may I ask? Vanished into the blue, she did; never come near me, nor wrote to me since – her own sister. Of course Hewitt did away with her – him and his jealous temper! – he threatened to do it, and do it, he did! And you coppers are so damn stupid that it takes you thirty-odd years to come around to seeing something that I was trying to knock into your thick heads within a few weeks of it happening.'

Rees opened the envelope on his lap and took out the pack of half-plate photographs.

'I'd like you to look at these, if you will, and tell me if you recognize any of them. They are pictures of some things we found with the body. They're badly knocked about. So, before I show them to you, can you give me some idea of the sort of clothes and jewellery that Mavis used to wear?'

The woman looked at him suspiciously. 'What do you want to know?'

'Well, what was she wearing when you last saw her, for a start?'

Jessie considered this for a moment. 'I told all this to the police at the time,' she repeated. 'I can't remember now. I think it was a green linen two-piece and a white blouse.'

'What sort of ornaments did she wear?'

Again the old woman looked at him warily, afraid that he was trying to catch her out.

'She had all sorts of things – everything that was in fashion in those days. A very smart girl, my poor Mavis was.' She dabbed her eyes, again with the soiled handkerchief.

'What kind of wedding ring did she have?'

'Just ordinary gold,' replied the sister evasively. 'A good one, mind you.'

'Do you know where it was bought?'

'No – down in Wales, I suppose. Hewitt must have got it from somewhere.'

'Did she normally carry a purse with her?'

Jessie looked scornfully at him. 'Of course she did. What woman doesn't?'

Rees selected a photograph and handed to her.

'Those are some glass beads we found. Did your sister have any like that?'

Jessie Randall fumbled in her apron again for her glasses and put them on. She looked at the photo for a brief moment and then handed it back. 'They're hers all right!' she announced smugly.

Rees looked at her with doubt plain on his face.

'Well, let's say that they are like some beads she had. Is that right?'

'Of course it's right! It's her poor body you found, so those are bound to be her beads. Stands to reason, doesn't it?'

Rees sighed. He had a sudden vision of defending counsel making mincemeat of her evidence in court, if it was all going to be on this level of inverted logic.

He handed her another picture. 'Those are some wooden beads. Do you recognize the type?'

Mrs Randall was more cautious this time. 'She had all sorts of things, did Mavis, bless her. I know she had wooden beads like this. They were very fashionable about that time.'

Willie passed over another print. 'And these – what about bits of chain like that?'

The old sister nodded energetically. 'Oh, yes, she used

to wear a chain around her neck quite often, with a locket on it – very popular they were, too. Had a picture of our dear mother in it – passed away when Mavis was fifteen. A mercy that she was spared seeing what happened to her daughter.'

With a feeling of increasing frustration, the detective went through all the bits and pieces found in the mine shaft and discovered that Jessie was willing to swear to all of them as being actually, or potentially, her sister's property. He came to the last one, that of the purse clasp. 'What about that.' He handed the photo over.

The woman sniffed scornfully. 'Just a purse fastener, isn't it – one's the same as the next.'

Rees gave up and put his pictures away.

'Have you got a photograph of Mavis that we could borrow for a short time?' he asked.

'I suppose I have,' the sister answered ungraciously.

'And do you think you could find those letters for us, as well. They would be most important and helpful to us, you see.'

She got up and slouched to the door. 'If it helps to put that old devil where he belongs, you're welcome to them. It's only a pity that you didn't get around to it years ago.'

She went off into the depths of the house and Rees heard drawers being opened and slammed shut.

Jessie Randall came back clutching a faded chocolate box, bulging with tattered letters and old birthday cards. After a lot of searching, she produced an old envelope and handed it to Willie.

'There you are. I kept them as the last thing I ever heard of my poor little sister.'

Rees took the envelope and removed several sheets of brittle notepaper from it. He quickly scanned through them and picked out some of the sentences, written in a large, childish hand. Satisfied with the importance of the find, he carefully put the envelope into his breast pocket.

'Thank you, Mrs Randall. I'll give you a receipt for this and the photograph.'

She passed him a frayed but quite clear snap of an attractive young woman, in a hat and hairstyle strange to the modern eye. This was Mavis Hewitt, and Willie Rees at once saw that it was a much better picture than the one in the Aberystwyth newspaper.

He smoothed out the sheets of paper on his knee. 'Now, if you don't mind, I'd like to take down what you've told me as a proper statement.'

Willie Rees' voice, and the grumbling of Jessie at repeating the same thing at thirty-year intervals, droned through the room while the rain beat ceaselessly at the windows.

The thread of evidence was being woven slowly around Roland Hewitt.

Chapter Ten

Extra chairs had been brought into the chief constable's office for the conference on the Wednesday morning. A half-circle of men sat around his wide desk, which was brightly lit by a shaft of sunshine coming through one of the windows overlooking the main shopping street of Cardigan town.

Colonel Barton shuffled his papers into order as the others waited in expectant silence.

For someone who only wants to be an observer, thought Charles Pacey, *he's doing a pretty heavy job of organizing*. The colonel finished fiddling with his notes and cleared his throat to command their already-undivided attention.

'Right, gentlemen, it's three days now since the first bone was found. I think we should be quite pleased at the progress so far, eh? Of course, as I've told Mr Pacey here, I'm only holding a watching brief on all this ...'

'Oh, Gawd, here he goes again!' muttered the superintendent.

'... but I thought it might be as well if we all met here today to recapitulate the results and see how we stand. I'd like to thank Professor Powell and Inspector Meadows for coming up from Swansea at such short notice.'

The pathologist smiled blandly in acknowledgement. He and Pacey sat directly in front of the chief constable and ranged on either side were Inspectors Meadows, Rees, and Morris from Aberystwyth, Sergeant Mostyn and the detective constable who did the photography. Also present on the end of the row was an old man with a poker-straight back and a white walrus moustache.

'I'd also like to thank ex-inspector Matthews for tearing himself away from his roses in New Quay, to come up and help with what he remembers about the case in twenty-nine,' concluded the colonel. The retired police officer nodded silently.

Barton turned to the pathologist. 'Perhaps you would like to start, Professor. To get straight down to brass tacks, we all know now that the best candidate for this body is Mavis Hewitt – she certainly leads the field so far, at any rate. Now how far can the medical evidence go towards proving this?'

Leighton Powell leaned forwards in his chair and rubbed his hands together thoughtfully.

'I don't know much about the real Mavis yet – I'm hoping to learn a lot more here this morning. But this is what she'll have to measure up to, to fit in with our skeleton.'

He began to tick off the points on his fingers.

'One – a woman between the ages of twenty-two and thirty. Those limits are quite definite. But I'd be inclined to think that she's at least a couple of years above the lower figure, say twenty-five. I couldn't be as dogmatic as that in the witness-box – but God preserve me from ever having to do that!'

He prodded the next finger.

'Five foot four in height. But, if Mavis was known to be an inch different either way, I'd accept that. All the same, if she was more than five-five or less than five-three, I'd rule her right out.'

Pacey broke in with a question: 'Can you say anything about her probable build? You know, fat, thin or indifferent?'

'No, sorry. The bones are just the same in either case. The only other thing I can tell you is that she was free from any bone disease, or deformity. There's the hair, of course, but Inspector Meadows can tell you more about it than I can.'

He settled back in his chair as if to indicate that he had shot his forensic bolt.

The chief looked at the laboratory liaison officer.

'Perhaps you'd like to carry on from there, Meadows.'

The inspector had his own sheaf of papers to ruffle through.

'We've not had nearly enough time to do anything but a very sketchy examination, sir. It will take a couple of weeks to do everything properly, but I can tell you a few things already that might be quite helpful.'

His manner slipped back into the formal stilted speech of the witness box. 'Several coins were examined, as follows: a florin, dated nineteen twelve, a nineteen twenty-seven shilling and three pennies, dated from nineteen twenty-one to six. There was also a plain brass purse clasp with no features of any use in tracing its origin.'

The colonel stopped him with a raised finger. 'What about fingerprints?'

Meadows looked slightly shocked. 'Oh, no, sir, not a hope! All the metal objects had a thick layer of corrosion on them. No dabs would survive that amount of time and ill-treatment.'

The colonel accepted the mild rebuke gracefully and Meadows carried on. 'One part of a shoe was compared with our records of costumes and with the collection in the National Museum. It was typical of the decade nineteen twenty-five to thirty-five. It had a pointed toe in leather, with, a button-strap across the instep. If we really push it, we might be able to get some manufacturer to give us a closer date on the time it was made.'

'How will that help?' asked Powell.

'Well, if it was made in thirty-one, it can hardly be Mavis. The next stuff we looked at was the jewellery. The glass beads are characteristic of a style common in the same period as the shoe. It's impossible to date it more accurately. That goes for the wooden beads, too.'

'And the wedding ring,' added the colonel.

'Yes, a plain twenty-two carat gold band. Hallmarked in London in nineteen twenty-three. Nothing else special about it.'

'Twenty-three, that's a bit early, isn't it?' objected Pacey. 'She was married in twenty-seven, wasn't she?'

Meadows shrugged. 'Either it was second-hand, or had been hanging about the shops or wholesalers for a couple of years. I'll make inquiries about it, if you like, but I don't think it would sink our theory just by being too old.'

'What about the clothing – and there was a bit of chain, too?'

'The chain was plated – rolled gold on brass. I've hawked it around to a goldsmith, but he couldn't help much. He said that they've made that stuff in the same way for years. The clothing was pretty tatty – pieces of brown linen and part of what could be a cambric blouse, which was white once. This had mother-of-pearl buttons, some loose and some still sewn on to the cloth. They are genuine mother-of-pearl, which is very unusual these days. Now they're all synthetic.'

'What are you going to do with these things – get some more work done on them?' asked Barton.

'Yes, some stuff has already gone off. The research labs of the big textile firms are very helpful. They're hot stuff at recognizing fibres – they might be able to date this cloth and even say where it was made. That goes for the buttons, too. We've sent one off to see if the commercial experts can give us any information about it.'

'Professor Powell said you had something to tell us about the hair – is that right?'

'Yes, I was coming to that next. There was a hair clasp, too. I almost forgot that. Again it was a genuine old tortoiseshell. They're all plastic these days. The hair itself – well, that was auburn, natural colour, no dye in it. It had been artificially waved, though only a trace was left in it by the time we examined it. As the professor has said, the funny thing was that all the ends were cut ends – no roots present at all.'

Pacey frowned. He leant back in his chair until it creaked dangerously and stared fixedly at Meadows.

'What's that mean? That whoever did her in, also cut off all her hair as well?'

Powell came back into the discussion:

'He might well have done – we've got the partly sawn-off arm, remember; that was one attempt at concealment. He might well have started to cut off all the hair with some notion of delaying, or defeating, identification.'

'Wouldn't there be signs of the hair roots left in the scalp?' asked the colonel.

'No, I would be very surprised to find any recognizable roots with the soft tissues destroyed as completely as they were. If the head were cropped short of hair, the roots would have vanished when the scalp rotted.'

Pacey came back to the sawn arm bone. 'We haven't heard much about this sawing, Professor – what are your ideas about it?'

'Not much to it that helps. The bone was sawn half across, as you saw, about three inches below the shoulder joint. Alongside it was a small cut, presumably an abortive attempt before the other.'

'And you think that this was an abandoned attempt at dismembering the body before trying to dispose of it?'

Powell inclined his head. 'Yes, sawing up corpses is almost a classical occupation amongst murderers! Ruxton was the most wholesale "cutter-upper" of recent years, but plenty of others have had a go at it. This chap seems to have given it up as soon as he saw what a mess he was making. Even though there's no circulation in a corpse, the blood tends not to clot after death, so there would still be an embarrassing lot of blood about.'

The dapper colonel folded his hands neatly on his blotter. 'Then we agree so far, that there is nothing in the medical evidence to rule out Mavis Hewitt?'

He looked around the ring of faces and collected the nods and grunts of assent.

'Now, Mr Pacey, what can you tell us about the other side of things? As this skeleton could be Mavis Hewitt, have you anything to suggest that it really is her?'

Pacey produced an envelope, which he handed across the desk. 'Inspector Rees interviewed her sister yesterday. She's now sixty-one – which is about four years older than Mavis would have been now – always assuming she's dead!' he added mischievously.

'There are two letters in the envelope, which she gave to the police at the time they reported her missing. Presumably, they figured in the report that was made at the time – by the way, sir, there's no trace of that anywhere, so we can give up any hope of seeing it now. Inspector Matthews here is our only link with nineteen twenty-nine, except for the bit in the station Occurrences book.'

Colonel Barton was scanning through the large immature writing on the faded blue notepaper.

'Most of this is sheer rubbish, but some parts are good evidence of really bad feeling between the two Hewitts,' he commented. 'If this is true, there was certainly some physical disagreement during the weeks before she vanished.'

Pacey wagged his large head. 'Especially that bit where she says that Hewitt threatened to stop her seeing Lloyd, or anyone else, for good.'

'Still, this doesn't make the old boy out to be a murderer,' complained the chief. 'These bits like "... when he got mad at me he punched me on the floor ..." and "... I lost my temper and then he bruised me and tore my dress ..." – they are fine for establishing the state of mind between the husband and wife. But, without definite evidence of identity and some suspicious actions on Hewitt's part, we'd never be able to charge him with murder.

'We've just got to keep scraping around until we accumulate enough circumstantial evidence to satisfy the DPP that a charge of murder might be made to stick. I'm inclined to think that those letters ring true. It's not really the sort of thing she'd concoct as a preliminary to bringing a divorce action.'

Barton looked across at the retired inspector, who had sat silent and attentive until now.

'Inspector Matthews, can you throw any light on the business from what you remember?'

'I was a sergeant at Aberystwyth in those days, sir,' he answered in a deep firm voice. 'Not the station sergeant, but we all knew most of what went on from day to day. This Hewitt business was quite a fuss for a time, but it soon died down after the papers lost interest. That Sunday paper was the cause of a lot of interest. It ran an article on the case a few weeks after it was reported – sensational type of thing, nothing new in it at all.'

'Do you remember seeing the sister?'

'Oh, yes, she was in and out of the station like a hopping jinny for a few days. She stayed here for a bit, making a damn nuisance of herself, asking why we weren't doing anything to find Mavis.'

'What *was* being done, anyway?'

'The inspector there went out to see Roland Hewitt several times, as the sister was pestering him. Hewitt just kept telling him that he knew nothing at all about his wife's disappearance, and that he cared even less. He came into the station one day for the inspector to take down a statement from him. But, as far as I heard, his story was always the same. His wife, he said, used to go off with other men and that, as far as he knew, that's where she was then.'

'He seemed quite indifferent, then, to the fact that she had left him?' asked Pacey.

'I only had it second-hand, of course, but that was the impression I had. And he kept saying that she hadn't vanished; for all he knew, she might come back the next day. This was all within a couple of weeks of the sister coming there to play the devil about it, you see. I had the feeling that Hewitt had had just about enough of his wife and wasn't fussy about having her found at all. He never made any move to do anything, or even to ask us how we were getting on with our investigations.'

The colonel looked at Pacey and raised his eyebrows significantly.

'Had you ever seen Mavis Hewitt yourself?' Pacey asked hopefully.

'No. Tremabon was way off my track, Superintendent.'

'What was done by your inspector, to look for the woman?' inquired the colonel.

The old police officer frowned in an effort to remember. 'The usual. We notified all local stations. Then, of course, we circulated her description to the other Welsh police forces and, I think, to Liverpool and the Metropolitan boys.'

The colonel turned back to Pacey.

'What about this Sunday newspaper – have we traced that?'

The burly detective produced a photostat from his own pile of documents. 'Here it is – dated a month after the one in the Aberystwyth paper – nothing at all in it. Just an over-embroidered rehash of the first story, with the same picture of Mavis and a photo of Bryn Glas Farm.'

'That was the place where they lived at the time, was it?' Meadows threw in this question as he craned his neck to look at the picture.

'Yes, it's almost opposite the place where he has a

cottage now, only on the other side of the road.'

'I had a look at it yesterday,' said Morris. 'It's way off the main road up towards the cliffs. The track to it carries on up past it until it peters out in the moorland ... not a hedge or house between it and the place where the bones were found.'

There was a moment's silence while this was digested.

'Again, that means nothing in itself,' the colonel said briskly, 'I'll admit there are a lot of suggestive circumstances here – but nothing yet that would induce the Director of Public Prosecutions to touch it with a bargepole. Now, Rees, what have you got to tell us about your visit to Liverpool, apart from these letters?'

The lanky inspector gave an account of his meeting with Jessie Randall. 'She definitely identified the ring and all the jewellery as belonging to Mavis. But, personally, sir, I wouldn't give tuppence for her evidence. She was as biased as she possibly could be. All she wants is old Hewitt's blood. She'd perjure herself from here to hell and back to see him charged with Mavis's murder. I don't think we should put much reliance on anything she says.'

'I quite agree,' supported Pacey. 'The only useful things she did were to hand over these letters and the photograph.'

'What are we going to do with that photo, Pacey?' said Barton. 'You said something about asking Professor Powell about it.'

The forensic pathologist wriggled himself up in his chair. 'Yes, I've had a chat with our photographer here, and he's going to knock up a superimposition for us. The picture is far better than that one from the newspaper. Again, it's nothing like conclusive. But it may at least disprove the identity – it can never actually prove it, I'm afraid.'

The colonel looked puzzled. 'I'm not quite with you here, Professor. What exactly are you going to do?'

'The constable here is going to make a full-plate enlargement of the photo of Mavis. Then he'll print a photo of the skull we found on transparent film, enlarging it to exactly the right degree, to correspond with the picture of the face. Then we put the skull film on top of the photo and staple it in place, with as exact an alignment as we can manage. Then we will be able to see how well various features, like nose, eyes and chin, will correspond.'

'Sounds an excellent idea to me,' enthused the colonel.

The photographer was less optimistic.

'It's difficult to get exactly the same angle on the skull as the photo was taken. This one's not so bad – it's almost dead full-face. But, still, it's a rough-and-ready business.'

Powell confirmed this, emphasizing the faults.

'Yes, this is only a rough guide. It can give the main proportions of the features – distance between the eyes, width of the cheekbones and things like that. But, of course, we can never know exactly how much must be allowed for the soft tissues on the face. If they are utterly unlike, we can say that it's unlikely to be Mavis. If they are alike, well, then, it could be her – but no more than that.'

'I seem to remember this being done in a famous murder case before the war,' observed the retired inspector.

'Yes, the Ruxton case,' said Powell. 'A doctor threw the dismembered pieces of his wife and maid over a bridge. The superimposition method was helpful there. And, ever since, pathologists have been trying to repeat the success, without much being achieved, I'm afraid.'

The conference seemed suddenly to have run dry of inspiration, and the colonel canvassed for more ideas.

'Anything else, anyone? What about you, Superintendent?'

'Nothing that matters. We've been through the village,

and there's nothing useful there. Plenty of gossip, but no hard facts. The old inhabitants who remember Mavis are unanimous in calling her a "fast baggage" but they still think that Hewitt did her in. Some say that she had it coming to her, carrying on with Ceri Lloyd as she did, and having dirty weekends up in Liverpool!'

Pacey's manner had a slightly flippant air about it and his chief's eyebrows came down in a frown.

'What about this man Lloyd? Don't think he's involved, do you?'

'Shouldn't think so for a minute. Anyway, we are going to have a hell of a job to nail this on to old Hewitt with the amount of evidence we've scraped together so far, let alone try to incriminate Lloyd – we've got nothing at all against him.'

The colonel was undecided as to whether or not Pacey was gently needling him. He switched his questions to Rees.

'Inspector, you've been looking into the "missing persons" angle, I believe. Any other possibilities there?'

'No, sir, not much joy. There was no central information about missing persons then. But I've checked all our county records, and there was no one else besides Mavis Hewitt reported missing between nineteen twenty-eight – the latest date on the coins – and nineteen thirty-two, who could possibly fit the range of age, or size, of our skeleton.'

'The body could have been brought from some other county,' objected the colonel.

Pacey grunted and shook his head. 'I doubt it, sir. And, even if it was, there must have been some close tie-up with the locality. Either the murderer, or the deceased, must have been from the area. Otherwise they wouldn't have known about the ideal place for hiding the body – that lead mine, facing out to sea, with a convenient ledge to park the corpse, was no accidental find. And, as the body got there around the late twenties or early thirties, my simple mind can't help stringing all the facts together into the conclusion that Roland Hewitt is the chap we want. Convincing a jury is another matter, of course.'

After this long speech, he settled back in his chair as if to indicate that his case rested and the others could take it or leave it.

'Mmm. Put like that, I'm inclined to agree with you,' said the colonel, playing with his inkstand. 'But are we going to get enough to charge him? Professor Powell, do you think that any further work on your part will get us nearer to proving that this was actually Mavis Hewitt?'

'Not a lot, Colonel. Tying up loose ends may narrow down the range of her age a little. But I can never prove that it's Mavis. The teeth might have been a way of doing that. But as there's no dental work on the teeth of the skull, and we've no dental record of the real Mavis, that's a washout.

'And does that hold for your laboratory too, Meadows?'

The liaison officer looked as doubtful as Powell.

'I'm afraid so. All we can do is narrow down the date of death by investigating the objects found with the body. We can never get a positive identification; there was nothing distinctive enough to be recognized by anyone.'

Colonel Barton fingered his moustache thoughtfully. 'Well, Pacey, where do you go from here?'

The superintendent noticed that the 'we' had changed to 'you', as the trail appeared to have petered out. He was being passed the buck, now that it was stone dead.

'I think we're stumped as far as substantive evidence goes,' he said. 'The scent has gone cold – thirty years cold! The only hope of getting on now – unless you think it's worth chancing our arm on this circumstantial stuff – is to get the old boy to confess. Or, at least, to work him over until he gets so harried and flustered that he drops a clanger.'

The colonel looked pained.

'I think your choice of words is unfortunate, Mr Pacey. We have to be very careful in our methods these days. Relations with the public are not too good, as it is. This proposed Chicago-style third degree sounds most unsavoury to me.'

'Yes, sir,' Pacey said meekly. He couldn't be bothered to argue.

The chief constable stood up to indicate that the meeting was at an end.

'Well, thank you, gentlemen, we'll have to wait now for some more developments, either from the laboratory or from Superintendent Pacey's efforts.'

The meeting broke up and eventually, Pacey found himself back in his own bare office with Willie Rees. He flung himself into his protesting swivel chair and began stuffing coarse tobacco into a pipe.

'Willie, the chief is a good stick, but sometimes he gets on my wick! All that guff about not interfering and then niggling about me wanting to get stuck into old Hewitt. I'd better get up there again this afternoon, I suppose. A pity, really. I quite like old Hewitt, even if he did try to saw his wife's arm off!'

'If you're going to work him over,' Rees said dryly, 'I'd better put the bright lights and rubber hosepipe in the back of your car!'

Chapter Eleven

Once again, Peter was out when the police called to see his uncle for the second time. Pacey and Rees spent an hour at the cottage on this occasion, the superintendent making Roland go over and over the events of the weeks before Mavis vanished, until the old chap's head was buzzing.

Persistently repeating his questions, Pacey harried Hewitt without a pause, trying to catch him out in some fact or to goad him into saying something that could be construed as incriminating.

Although, by the end of the hour, Roland had reached such a state of confusion that he hardly knew himself what he was saying, the detectives had to go away having made no real progress at all.

Pacey's only hope was that his badgering and insinuations, with half-veiled promises of new information just around the corner, would work on the old man's mind so much that their next session of questioning might be more fruitful.

'That didn't get us very far, Willie, did it?' he said ruefully as they bumped down the track away from the cottage.

'He's got such a simple story to stick to, hasn't he?' replied the inspector. 'He says he doesn't know what happened to her. She went out one day and never came back – end of story! Nothing to trip him up on at all.'

Pacey swore under his breath. 'But, damn it, he *must* have done it, the old fox! There can't be any other answer. They have rows and fights – no one disputes that – she vanishes, and a body uncommonly like hers turns up not a mile away from the farm! No one else could or would want to do her in. I've got a feeling that unless he cracks and spills the beans next time we see him, we've had it. The DPP won't indict him on the evidence we've got so far, even though it is good solid circumstantial stuff.'

The two disappointed policemen drove away, missing Peter's car at the entrance to the lane by only a couple of minutes.

He got back to the cottage to find his uncle in a desperate state of agitation, marching up and down the kitchen floor, mumbling to himself.

As soon as his nephew appeared, he rushed towards him, hands outstretched. 'They've been here again, boy – the police!' he almost babbled. 'Hours and hours, they've been at me – questions, questions, questions – I've had enough of it! As good as told me they know I killed her, they did.'

Peter tried to calm him down, but Roland had worked himself into a state of panic.

'They'll be coming for me any time now, boy,' he said desperately, his watery eyes rolling behind his glasses. '"New evidence", they said they were waiting for – the fat one told me that. They'll arrest me as soon as they've got it, you wait and see, boy.'

'Look, I've told you before, Uncle, this is all part of the police game – to frighten you into saying something that will incriminate you. And, as you've got nothing to say, you'll be all right.'

'I don't know, boy. I don't know! I'm frightened, that's for sure. I should never have come back here. I should have stayed in Canada.'

Roland calmed down after a few minutes gentle talking-to and a cup of the inevitable tea. Peter sat down with him in the kitchen and began to talk seriously about what should be done.

'I think you were right yesterday, it's time we had a

lawyer in on this – if only to protect you from the police overstepping the mark with their questions.'

'But they can do what they like, boy. They as good as said they knew I was the guilty one when they were here.'

'Don't you believe it, Uncle, I fancy that Pacey has gone too far already. They depend on people not knowing their rights. There are things called Judges' Rules that stop the police from questioning people once they expect to arrest them, and then as soon as they do arrest them, they have to caution them that they needn't say any more if they don't want to.'

As soon as the words were out of his mouth, Peter saw that he had said the wrong thing. Roland became excited and slapped the table with his hand.

'Well there, boy, you're saying yourself now that they're expecting to arrest me. They must know that this here skeleton belongs to Mavis, otherwise they wouldn't be making such a dead set for me.'

Peter tried vainly to make up the ground he had lost, but Roland became progressively more jumpy and nervous. He started meandering around the room again, rubbing his hands.

'Perhaps I'd better go back to Canada. I've got enough money. I could go tomorrow, out of the way,' he said wildly. 'They'll have me if I stay here, I know they will.'

His nephew began to fear for the old fellow's sanity for a moment. Roland had always been slightly eccentric, isolated and withdrawn. Peter had assumed that this was a result of living for most of his life alone and away from his home and family. Now that this crisis had burst upon him, Peter was afraid that the combination of his oddness and his age might unhinge him altogether.

'I'll tell you what I'm going to do, Uncle,' he said firmly,

'I'm going down to Carmel House and ask Doctor John or one of the boys to come up and see you. You need something for your nerves – or something to give you a good night's sleep at the very least.'

Roland subsided into a limp pathetic figure, slumped into his chair. 'All right, boy, there's nothing I can do, except wait for those police to come again.'

'And, first thing in the morning, I'm going to see that solicitor of yours in Aberystwyth and get his advice.'

Peter stayed with his uncle for an hour or so until Roland had settled back into a gloomy but calmer frame of mind. Then he drove down to the doctor's house and told Mary of the old man's distress.

'I'll ask Daddy to go up and see him after supper. You can leave him long enough to stay with us for a meal, can't you?' she pleaded.

Peter thought that his holiday, intended to be a couple of weeks of blissful idleness with his fiancée, was turning out to be a nightmare. He was torn between leaving Roland alone and spending some time with Mary; but, salving his conscience with the thought that one of the doctors would be going up to see the old man, he agreed to stay to supper. Mary's father and both her brothers were in for the meal, which, as was to be expected, turned into a discussion about Roland's troubles.

'I suppose Pacey is only doing his job, but he's pushing Uncle Roland a bit too hard to be legitimate, I think,' said Peter, as they were having coffee.

'But they can never prove that it is Mavis's body, surely?' objected David, his pointed chin jutting out in indignation. 'However much they think it is, they've a devil of a job to prove it. And, until they do, your uncle can't possibly be charged with murder, or anything else, can he?'

'But perhaps they can prove it,' said Gerald, his face as worried as if his own father were being accused. His usual banter had deserted him, just as David's normally serious manner had become almost funereal.

'How can they?' asked his father.

'We don't know what's been going on since Sunday,' went on the younger brother. 'The police have had their pathologist and their laboratory on the go. For all we know, they might have discovered something that could clinch the identity of the body. It might even be a blind, all this about Mavis Hewitt; they might have ideas about someone else. Have you heard anything at all, Peter, with your newspaper contacts?'

Peter shook his head. 'No, I've kept well clear. I'm in a rather embarrassing spot, having a sort of obligation to the *Morning News*, and to my uncle at the same time. Nothing has appeared in any of the papers. I can't imagine how Pacey fobbed off our man from Pembroke.'

John Ellis-Morgan tapped his spoon in the saucer with nervous persistence that jarred on Mary's ears.

'Gerald is right,' he said. 'We've no idea how much the police know about the body – though I can hardly imagine any reason for them worrying old Roland if they genuinely don't believe the skeleton to be that of his wife.'

'If only I could do something to fault their theory,' burst out Peter in sudden frustration. 'I know they've got all the experts and facilities, but they're more interested in finding facts to prove that the body is Mavis, rather than eliminating her.'

The elder doctor flicked his eyes around to Peter.

'Oh, come now, I don't think they're biased in any way. They'd accept any genuine facts, whether that helped their case or not.'

'I didn't mean that. I know they wouldn't weigh the issue one way or the other. But, surely, their efforts will be concentrated on finding positive facts about the similarities between the two. I wondered if, with my Press connections, I could dig up anything that would show that the real Mavis had something distinctive about her that would knock a hole in the police case.'

'Darling, I don't see what you could possibly do. The police have all the advantages, surely?'

'You're thinking of finding some abnormality like a healed fracture in the real Mavis, is that it?' David spoke from across the table and Peter was again reminded that he was a younger edition of his father, in both looks and manner.

'I suppose so. But, to tell you the truth, I'm not at all clear myself. I'm just mad keen to do something to help the old boy. If you'd have seen him this afternoon, you'd have sworn that the police were waiting outside with handcuffs, he was that convinced that he was on the point of being arrested.'

Gerald brought the conversation back to a practical level.

'But there's nothing to suggest that Mavis *did* have a fracture, is there?'

David gestured at him impatiently. 'I didn't mean it literally, Gerry. I was just giving that as an example. Anyway, the Home Office chap would have sorted that out long ago.'

'It would have to be in the bones, this fault of yours, Peter. No abnormality in the flesh would be any good,' said John Ellis-Morgan.

'I remember reading in a book about Spilsbury that an old operation scar was vitally important in the Crippen case,' offered Mary.

'That's what Dad has just said, Mary,' snapped David. 'Nothing in the skin would be the slightest use.'

'What about the teeth?' asked Peter.

'I'm sure the police pathologist would have flogged that one already,' said Gerry. 'I remember looking at the skull. There was no dental work or any fillings at all. Lots of the teeth were missing, in fact.'

'It's useless trying to think of things sitting here, Peter,' the father said gently. 'I should ask your uncle if he can remember any detail, however small, about his wife that may help. I'm afraid I don't see much chance of finding anything, but you never know.'

'Daddy, you're going up to see him this evening. You could ask him. You might have a better idea about fractures and medical things than Peter has.'

John Ellis-Morgan departed for the old man's cottage after supper, leaving the four younger people in an uneasy mood. .

'I've, heard a lot of rumour in the village these past few days, Peter,' David said grimly, tapping the end of a cigarette with the same jerky movements as his father. 'Almost every patient who comes into the surgery has a natter about old Hewitt. The older ones, who remember Mavis, are unanimous in saying that she was a bad lot.'

'I've had the same thing,' confirmed Gerry. 'No one seems to have any doubt that Roland did it. And they seem to be sorry for him. Apparently, everyone was astounded when he came back from Canada five years ago ... they

thought he'd hopped it to avoid the scandal and died over there years ago.'

'Yes, I understood that everyone thought he was dead,' said David. 'I heard rumours about a missing wife and some dark secret in Roland's past, long before all this fuss blew up.'

'You didn't say anything about it before!' cried Mary, indignant that her brother should have kept some local gossip to himself.

'It didn't occur to me on Sunday to connect the bones in the old mine with the missing Mavis,' replied David. 'I assumed that they were real antiques, as Gerry thought. It's only the local scandalmongers that have put the idea into our heads – and the heads of the police, too, no doubt.'

A futile discussion went on for a long time, Mary even suggesting that the corpse was wrapped in a dated newspaper which had given the police a clue as to its origin!

'Talking of newspapers, did you manage to look up that old copy of the Aberystwyth paper, Peter?' asked David.

'I went up there yesterday, but the assistant manager said that the police had taken the file for the whole of that period.'

'What about an inquest – there will have to be one, will there?' asked Gerald.

'I looked this up in the library yesterday, while I was up in Aber,' said Peter. 'Apparently, if an old or incomplete body is found, the coroner has to ask the Home Secretary's advice as to whether it's worth holding an inquest. I'm sure he will in this case. But, if there is any possibility of a criminal charge – poor old Roland in this case – then the inquest is only a formal affair of a few minutes. It has to be adjourned until the findings of the criminal court are known.'

The conversation revolved around Roland Hewitt and his troubles until John Ellis-Morgan came back from the cottage.

'He's not too bad now,' said the doctor when he came in. 'Worried and depressed, but quite sensible about the whole business. I've given him a couple of sleeping capsules, so he should have a good night's rest, if nothing else.'

'Thank goodness for that. He spent half last night walking up and down his bedroom. The creaking boards nearly drove me crazy.' As Peter spoke, he noticed that the elder doctor seemed even more twittery than usual.

'Peter, I don't want to raise your hopes for nothing,' began John Ellis-Morgan. 'But I asked Roland if he could think of anything special about Mavis's health. He came up with one little fact that, unlikely though it may be, could be worth following up.'

Peter, in spite of the caution, sat up eagerly.

'What was that? I don't care how feeble a chance it is, I'm ready to clutch at any straw.'

'Well, the first thing I asked him was about the teeth. But he said that, in the four years that he was with her, she had nothing done to them. And, as far as he knew, she had no fillings or extractions before that.'

'That doesn't help much,' objected Gerry. 'It makes it worse, in fact.'

'Wait a minute, lad, will you,' his father said with a grimace. 'Though there was nothing helpful in the teeth, and she certainly had no deformity of her bones, old Roland remembered that she'd had a small operation about six months after they were married.'

'But everyone shouted me down when I mentioned the Crippen operation,' objected Mary. 'So what's the use?'

Her father shook his fists in the air. 'Wait a minute, will you – what a set of children I've got! If you'd give me a chance to finish, I'd tell you that this was an operation on the nose, for sinus trouble.'

In spite of his father's outburst, David immediately raised more objections. 'But that's so trivial that it wouldn't leave any trace. It might even be only a drainage through the nostril!'

The elder physician became almost apoplectic. 'God give me patience! I was going to point out that X-rays of the skull are always taken before any sinus operation. Does that mean anything to you?'

There was a second's silence, then David breathed out noisily.

'Aah, the penny has dropped, Dad.'

Peter was still completely in the dark over this medical matter. 'I suppose I'm ignorant, but I don't see where this is going to help Uncle Roland.'

John Ellis-Morgan began to explain: 'If X-rays were taken of Mavis's head, and we could find them, they could be compared with the X-rays of the skull from up on the cliff. That would provide a hundred per cent sure check on the identity. No two skulls are identical, any more than fingerprints are.'

It was David's turn to be sceptical about the chances of success. 'You haven't got a hope in hell of finding those films, even if they were taken. I don't even know if X-rays were used for sinusitis in the twenties.'

The father wagged his head energetically. 'Oh, yes they were. I'd thought of that snag. But I distinctly remember seeing skull X-rays with opaque sinuses when I was a student – and that must have been before twenty-five, when I qualified.'

'But it's fantastic,' scoffed Gerry. 'You'd never get films thirty-odd years old. The hospitals normally chuck them out after seven years – or ten, at the most.'

'We don't even know where the operation was done,' added David.

'In Liverpool. I asked Roland that,' replied John, with a grin of triumph. 'She went up to stay with her sister for a few weeks and visited a private specialist there.'

Peter stood up, excited at the prospect of being able to do something, however nebulous, to help his uncle.

'It's worth a try – I'm going straight back to see if Roland can remember any more details. Then I'll go up to Liverpool in the morning and see this sister. She'll know something about it – she's bound to, if Mavis stayed with her at the time.'

'Sister? What sister?' asked Gerry in surprise.

'The same one that reported her missing all those years ago. The police told my uncle that she was still alive and helping them with their inquiries. If I ring up Pacey in the morning, I'm sure he'll give me her address. There's no reason why he should keep it dark.'

'Don't hope for too much, Peter,' warned Mary's father.

'In fact, don't hope at all, then you won't be so

disappointed. The chances of getting those films – if there ever were any – is almost nil, as Gerry said just now.'

As he moved with Mary to the door, Gerry had an even more serious warning for him.

'And remember, if you *do* find them, they might prove exactly the opposite of what you want – that the body definitely *does* belong to Mavis Hewitt!'

Chapter Twelve

Although it had stopped raining when Peter arrived in Liverpool, Glebe Terrace looked no less dismal to him than it had to Willie Rees a day or two earlier.

He found the address that he had wheedled out of Pacey and hammered on the front door. The same woman in the same drab outfit glowered at him across the doorstep.

When he explained who he was – the nephew of Roland Hewitt – she almost slammed the door in his face; but curiosity got the better of her and she heard him out while he explained what he wanted.

Her manner, never very sunny, became positively frigid. He thought for a moment that she was going to tell him nothing, but she must have felt so sure of the old man's guilt that she became almost arrogant.

'Well, young man, I think you must be mad coming all the way up here on a wild-goose chase. I can't see why you want to find out something that's only going to knock a few more nails into your uncle's coffin. Perhaps you're in a hurry to get something under his will, eh?'

Peter managed to control his feelings, and his tongue; for he knew that to antagonize her now would be to make his journey a complete waste of time.

'No, Mrs Randall, we just want to get at the truth, whichever way it lies. All I want to know is the name of the hospital where your sister had her sinus operation.'

The unattractive widow sniffed and wiped her hands on her apron. She was still standing in her doorway, not having invited Peter in out of the damp foggy air – as if to emphasize that any relation of Roland was unwelcome at her house.

For a long moment, she seemed undecided whether to tell him or not, and he stood with his pulses thumping in his temples while she made up her mind. At last, she gave in.

'Well, if you really want to know, it was the Chester Road Infirmary. Not that she went in as an ordinary patient, mind you – no National Health in those days. She went to a specialist first, who got her in there to one of his private wards. Only in a day, she was, anyway.'

Having got all the help he was going to have, Peter snapped a curt 'Thank you' and turned on his heel before she had a chance to slam the door in his face.

Back in the car, he drove to a nearby shop and, over the purchase of some cigarettes, asked the way to the Infirmary. His fears that the place might have been demolished, or blitzed out of existence, during the past thirty years were dispelled by the shopkeeper. A few minutes later he found himself outside a gaunt group of sooty red-brick buildings, fashioned in an atrocious Victorian style which made them look a cross between a workhouse and a public convenience.

In contrast, the inside was surprisingly bright and well-decorated. He followed the wall signs to the X-ray department and soon found himself in a neat office.

A white-coated girl behind the counter put out a hand for his form, thinking he was a patient.

'I'm trying to find some X-rays,' he explained. 'They're pretty old, I'm afraid. They belong to a patient who had a sinus operation many years ago.'

The girl seemed to assume that he was a doctor from another hospital and Peter didn't disillusion her.

'How long ago was it?'

'About the early part of nineteen twenty-seven. I've got her name and address if that would help you.'

The clerk looked amazed. 'The twenties! Oh, I'm sorry, we only keep films for ten years. We destroy them then, unless there's any special reason not to.'

Peter's heart sank. Although this was what he had expected, the final realization was bitter. It seemed that he'd fallen at the first fence.

The girl saw the look of disappointment on his face and decided that he must be writing some important medical article that depended on these X-rays being available.

'Doctor, there might be one faint hope. I remember that someone here wanted some very old films recently and he managed to get them from a private radiologist. Before the National Health Service, there were a lot of private specialists who did most of the X-ray work. Perhaps, if you tried one of them, you might strike lucky.'

Peter felt that he was really clutching at straws in the wind now, but asked how he could go about it.

'You'll have to get the case notes from Records Office – it would probably say in those who took the X-rays. They keep the notes much longer than we keep films, so I expect you'd get hold of them quite easily.'

Peter thanked her and set off on a long ramble through the white corridors to the Records Department.

He eventually came to another counter, facing another clerk, a middle-aged woman this time. He explained his errand, and the woman began to look worried. She had no illusions about his being a doctor.

'Well, sir, we've probably got the notes. But I couldn't possibly let you have them without the medical superintendent's permission – they're confidential and, naturally, only the medical staff are allowed to see them.'

Peter smiled reassuringly. 'Well, actually, I don't want to see them myself. All I want to know is whether they name the doctor who took some X-rays, so that I can try to trace them. Perhaps you would be good enough to do that without handing the notes over at all. I'm sure there can be no official objection to that.'

He gave her one of his appealing smiles which he found so useful when he was engaged in his journalistic encounters with the opposite sex, and the woman gave in.

'No, I can't see any harm in that. It'll take time to find them. They'll be down in the basement, if they're that old. Can you come back in an hour?'

Promptly at the arranged time, he was back at the counter, fortified with several cups of WVS coffee from the outpatients' buffet.

The records clerk handed him a slip of paper.

'You're in luck,' she said. 'At least, some X-rays of skulls were taken. There was a report from a private radiologist to the surgeon there. Your Mavis Hewitt must have attended the consulting rooms herself, as the report isn't one from the hospital itself.'

Peter's hopes soared, although he realized that the chances of the actual X-ray film still being in existence were very remote. He thanked the clerk warmly and rushed back to a public telephone in the outpatient's hall. He looked at the name on the slip of paper and rifled through the telephone book to try to find it.

'Stanton-Reid, Dr Nicholas, MD, 18 King's Heath Place.' He thanked heaven that it was an unusual name and doubled his thanks when he found the same name in the directory.

Then he saw that the name was 'Mrs Stanton-Reid.'

'Oh, hell, he must be dead!' he muttered. 'That's torn it. It must be his widow. But I may as well waste fourpence in satisfying myself, now that I've got this far.'

He dialled the number and a gentle female voice answered. Peter explained his mission again, saying that he was after some old X-rays taken by Dr Stanton-Reid.

'My husband has been dead for over ten years,' said the old lady in mild surprise.

Peter, in a mood of hopeless determination to see the

142

thing through to the bitter end, explained that he wanted some films, taken in nineteen twenty-seven, for legal purposes.

'Oh, as long ago as that? Well, I wonder ... I don't know for sure, but some of the very old ones may still be up in the attic. You see, my husband gave up his private work in the early thirties to go back to hospital. He brought all his records and files back to the house and dumped them in the attic. He was very particular about not having any of his things interfered with. And, as far as I know, they are still there.'

Peter's spirits zoomed up from the region of his boots. He asked excitedly whether he might come and look for the ones he needed.

Mrs Stanton-Reid gave him rough directions about how to reach King's Heath; and, twenty minutes later, he was outside the house. This was in one of the older and now slightly run-down upper class districts of Liverpool.

Like the district, the house had the air of affluent gentility gone to seed. A frail little woman of about seventy opened the door to him. He presented her with the details supplied on the sheet of Chester Road Infirmary notepaper – which seemed to satisfy the doctor's widow that he was not a 'conman' or thief. She led him up several flights of gloomy stairs, which smelt of camphor and old polish, to the attics.

The first room was filled with broken furniture and heaps of unidentifiable junk. Beyond this was another room with a sharply sloping ceiling, not quite as chaotic, but covered with a similar layer of dust and grime.

The old lady pointed out several heaps of brown paper parcels lying in the centre of the floor.

'There they are – never touched, as far as I know, since the day my husband left the consulting rooms.'

Peter rubbed some of the grey dust from the top bundle and found that the dates "1923-25" were pencilled on the paper. *The private practice couldn't have been very prosperous*, he reflected, *if that represents the total of two years' work*. He lugged the parcel off the ones beneath and looked at the date on the next. This was "1926-27".

With mounting excitement, he dragged it to the small window to get it in a better light.

The doctor's widow watched him silently as he snapped the rotten cords around the bundle. Peter wondered whether she was thinking of the days when her husband tied up the parcel, all those years before.

Praying that he wouldn't be defeated after getting so near to success, he peeled off the double layer of thick paper and exposed a great wad of black celluloid films. They were of all sizes, the biggest being about the area of a half-folded newspaper.

Peter found that the top ones were stuck firmly together by damp. When he tried to separate them, the black emulsion tore off in jagged sheets, each layer sticking to the next film.

He quickly checked the slip of paper from the hospital records. It bore the date "March the third, nineteen twenty-seven". The centre films were not sticking so badly as the outer, and he flicked through them to see the names and dates written in white ink in the corners. With a tight feeling in his stomach, he thumbed through the dates, which seemed to be in strict order.

'August, November, February,' he chanted to himself as the sheets flicked through his fingers, 'February the twenty-seventh, March the first, second ... third!' Now he concentrated on the names, written boldly in the corners of the black sheets.

'Roach, Wells, Smart, Hewitt ... Hewitt!'

He shouted the name and pulled out two medium-sized films, waving them in the air.

The little widow looked almost as pleased as he did himself. She had been watching closely and had shared in

144

the tense last stages of his search.

'This is wonderful, more than I dared hope for!'

He waved the films again, exultantly. 'Can I take them with me? I'll give you a receipt for them, if you wish?'

The old lady waved this aside. 'No, if they are the slightest use to you, keep them. They're of no value at all to anyone else.'

After more profuse thanks, Peter left the house and laid the X-rays reverently on the back seat of his car. He couldn't resist having a quick look at them, by holding them up to the light. He saw that they were, in fact, the side and front views of a skull. Just before driving off, he sobered up a little after his burst of high spirits, remembering David Ellis-Morgan's warning. The films might, within a few hours, confirm that the bones from the cliff were indeed those of his aunt, Mavis Hewitt.

'Oh, how the hell can they be?' he muttered, and let in the clutch for the long journey back to Tremabon and the moment of truth.

Chapter Thirteen

'Come on, Uncle, let's take these down to Carmel House and see what they think of them,' urged Peter, later that night. Even the long tiring journey back from Liverpool and the ever-present fear of clinching the identity as being that of Mavis, had failed to dampen his excitement at finding the X-rays.

'A bit late, isn't it, boy – nearly ten o'clock?' Roland was half-afraid of this new evidence. He wanted to share in his nephew's elation, but a deep mistrust of everything scientific made him reluctant to rely on these pieces of black celluloid as a means of releasing him from his fear of the police.

'No, it's not too late. Come on,' coaxed Peter, propelling Roland towards the cottage door and his waiting car. 'They're sure to be wondering what's happened. I promised to let them know as soon as I could.'

With the precious X-rays now wrapped up carefully in new paper, they drove the short distance to the house near the beach.

'We've got them!' shouted Peter, waving the films above his head as soon as Mary had opened the door. 'Two lovely skull pictures. These will fix friend Pacey. Then I'll be able to write something up for the *News* – the editor must be wondering what the hell's wrong with me.'

Half-carrying Mary by hugging her around the waist with his free arm, Peter made for the lounge where John Ellis-Morgan was watching television.

Mary broke away from him and ran to Roland. 'Oh, Mr Hewitt, I'm so glad, you must have had an awful time. Sit down and talk to Daddy, I'll make some coffee and call Gerry – he's writing something in the surgery.'

Peter told the senior doctor the story of his treasure hunt in Liverpool and gave him the X-rays to look at.

'I'm so glad you found them, Peter. And I'm sure this should take a weight off your mind, Mr Hewitt, eh?'

He held the films up close to the standard lamp and studied them closely. 'Front and side views – quite clear considering how old they are, what? I used to do a bit of radiology myself, before the war. We GPs used to help out in the local hospital in those days; but the war, and the Health Service, ruined all that. These pictures certainly show an opaque sinus on the left – not that that matters a bit, except to confirm that these are Mavis's X-rays.'

'Her name's in the corner,' pointed out Peter. 'And the date.'

'Ah, well the police can't argue with that. All that matters now is to make sure that these can be shown to be different from the skull from the south cliff – then all your troubles will be over, Mr Hewitt.'

Roland, sitting on the extreme edge of one of the doctor's chairs, blinked with emotion.

'I don't know how to thank you, Dr John. It was your idea – I hope to God that this will be the end of the business.'

The door opened and Gerald came in, his dark eyes glittering with anticipation.

'Peter, you've got them, then. Let's see, Dad. Evening, Mr Hewitt. I'll bet you were pleased to see these.'

He strode across the room and took the films from his father's hand, holding them up against the light again.

'Pretty fuzzy, aren't they?' he asked critically. 'Not much definition on them.'

His father bridled at this. 'They're very good, man! You young chaps don't know how well off you are. Those pictures were taken over thirty-five years ago, with the old "gassy" type tubes. You can't expect them to be as crystal clear as modern X-rays.'

'As long as they give old Pacey a good kick in the pants, I don't care how "gassy" they are, whatever that means!' Peter said happily. 'Uncle and I are off to beard him in his den in Cardigan, first thing in the morning. Pacey's not a bad chap, but I think he overdid the third degree business with Uncle. I won't be sorry to get a bit of my own back.'

'I suppose he must have had some good grounds, though,' commented John Ellis-Morgan. 'The bobbies don't go around grilling people for nothing, surely? Of course,' he added hastily, 'we all know that he was barking up the wrong tree. But, somewhere along the line, there must have been some misleading information that sent him after Mr Hewitt here.'

The old man nodded fervently. 'I was beginning to feel that I had done something awful by the time they finished with me. Something must have convinced them that it was me that was responsible for her disappearing.'

'Well, having a body turn up less than a mile from your old house was quite a coincidence, to be fair to Pacey,' said Gerald.

'Too much of a coincidence, perhaps,' said Peter thoughtfully.

Mary came back with coffee and biscuits and they sat eating and drinking, waiting for David to come back from a local call.

'I wonder where Mavis really is?' asked Mary. 'Wouldn't it have been a scream if they had arrested Mr Hewitt here and then she had turned up waving a newspaper! The police would look real charlies, wouldn't they?'

Roland shook his head sadly. 'No, I think she must be dead, Miss Mary. She couldn't have stayed as quiet as this all these years. I knew her too well. She was much too

149

keen on her rights and her share of my money to have stayed away for long. That's partly why I've been afraid. I knew she must be dead and feared that this body could well have been hers, even though I had nothing to do with it getting there.'

John Ellis-Morgan jumped out of his chair, like a sparrow hopping off a branch, and stood with his back to the fire.

'I wouldn't worry about that, Mr Hewitt. I'm sure these X-rays will show that the body is that of someone quite different. You and Peter here will convince the detectives in the morning and it'll be plain sailing after that. As long as that wasn't Mavis up in the mine, it doesn't matter two hoots where she is now. I don't think you care much yourself, do you?'

Roland sighed. 'No indeed. Any feelings I ever had for her vanished before she did herself. I would have left her, or divorced her, before long, if this hadn't happened. That's what has been making it look so bad for me, you see.'

There was a scrunching of tyres on the gravel outside and the sound of a car door slamming.

'Here's Dave now. I'll go and tell him the news.' Mary said. She ran out to open the door for him. In a moment, he appeared in the lounge, peeling off a short leather coat and driving gloves. Summer and winter, he insisted on driving an open Austin-Healey, only resorting to the hood in the very worst weather.

'A proper family gathering. Hello, Mr Hewitt.'

His father waved the X-rays at him.

'Success, David. Come and look at these. Peter has foiled the majesty of the law!'

David strode across the room to take the films.

'Well, well!' he breathed, after holding them to the light. 'You're committed now, Peter – for better or for worse.'

'Are you talking about us or the X-rays?' asked Mary in mock indignation, holding on to her fiancés arm.

'These, sis.' He waggled the films. 'You're going to risk showing them to the superintendent, are you?'

'What the dickens do you mean, David?' bristled his father. 'I hope you're not suggesting that they are likely to be the same as the skull.'

David flopped down into a vacant chair.

'Of course not – but will there be a recognizable difference? It would be awful to give the coppers something to strengthen their case, instead of cracking it – just because there was not enough to declare the two things were different.'

John Ellis-Morgan bobbed up and down on the tips of his toes.

'Look, son, you might have been a quack pathologist in Cardiff before you came into practice, but I was a quack X-ray wallah. And I'm telling you that the chances of getting two identical skull X-rays are nil! Think of all the different things that would have to coincide – the sinuses, the thickness of the vault, the shape of the vault, the pituitary, jaws, teeth and roots … impossible!'

This list convinced even the habitually pessimistic elder son, and the group in the lounge became cheerfully confident of success by the time Peter and Roland left for home.

Roland had a good night's sleep without tablets; and, next morning, they made an early start for Cardigan. They arrived at the police headquarters at nine o'clock and ran Pacey to earth in his office. As they were shown in, Inspector Rees entered through another door and stared curiously at Roland Hewitt, wondering what had brought him to the police. Pacey was standing behind his desk, ploughing through a heap of letters and messages.

'Morning to you, Mr Adams. And to you, Mr Hewitt … do sit down.' His tone was a little too hearty and

Peter thought that the detective looked uneasy.

'What can I do for you both?'

Roland was dressed in his best suit, which smelled strongly of mothballs. He sat gingerly on a hard chair and appeared to be waiting for Pacey to call someone to clap the handcuffs on his wrists.

The superintendent stood expectantly, a bland smile on his face. Peter was puzzled. After the repeated urgings he had made to Roland to come across with the truth, he expected Pacey to say something like, 'Have you come to make a statement, Mr Hewitt?'

Instead, the policeman waited behind his desk like a genial John Bull.

Peter produced his precious X-ray films and dropped them on the desk in front of Pacey.

'We came to give you these, Mr Pacey,' he said, failing to keep a trace of smug triumph from his voice. 'They are new evidence – for the defence,' he added facetiously.

Pacey picked them up, looked briefly at them and put them back on the desk.

'What are they?' he asked.

'X-ray films of the real Mavis Hewitt's skull. If your pathologist cares to compare them with the skull that was found in Tremabon, I'm sure that he'll have to tell you to forget all about Mavis Hewitt. And then you can stop pestering my uncle here.'

Pacey picked up the X-rays and held them out across the desk.

'OK, you win!' he said, 'I apologize for roughing you up a bit, Mr Hewitt, but I promise I'll never come near you again.'

He smiled broadly at Peter and then at his uncle.

Peter was dumbfounded. He glared at the superintendent. 'Look, I'm serious, I want you to keep those and give them to Professor Powell.'

'I'm serious too, Mr Adams. I've said I accept your

word. Actually, I'll keep these for now. Perhaps the professor would like to see them, for interest.'

'For interest!' exclaimed Peter. 'How do you know I'm not spinning you a yarn? What's the idea? You'll have to get them checked against the skull first.'

Pacey smiled gently at the journalist. 'It's all right, Mr Adams. I don't need convincing that your uncle had nothing to do with this affair. Thanks for your trouble, but I knew already that this woman wasn't Mavis Hewitt.'

Willie Rees, a silent spectator of the scene, looked sharply at his superior. He only just avoided letting his mouth fall open with surprise.

Pacey looked at his wristwatch. 'Look, I owe you some reward for messing you about, Mr Hewitt, so perhaps I can repay you through your nephew here. If you come back, in say an hour, Mr Adams, I can give you a bit of hot news that will go down well with your editor. I've tried to keep everything under cover so far, but something's broken this morning that should be a fair sensation. That suit you?'

Peter, bewildered but relieved beyond measure, nodded mutely.

Pacey galloped around the desk to shake Roland by the hand. 'Sorry again for all the trouble, old chap, but we had our job to do the best way we could. Now you go home and forget all about it. I'll see you about half past ten, Mr Adams. You'll have a clear twelve hours' lead on any other papers.'

As the door closed on the stupefied pair, Rees found his voice.

'Super, for God's sake, what was all that about? I thought we were due to go to Tremabon today, to work old Hewitt over again.'

Pacey lumbered back to his chair and dropped his dead weight into the protesting frame. He picked up one of the flimsy telephone message slips from the litter on his desk, and waved it at his assistant.

'This was waiting for me when I came in this morning.'
His voice rose in pitch a little. 'We've been had, Willie.
Some smart alec has led us right up the bloody garden path.'

He stood up suddenly and his long-suffering chair skidded backwards.

'Nineteen twenty-flaming-nine be damned!   ... look at this panic message from the forensic lab.'

He walked across to Rees with the form and poked him hard in the chest with a massive forefinger.

'See that? ... they say that one of the blouse buttons from that bleeding shaft was sewn on with Terylene thread! And Terylene thread wasn't on the market until at least nineteen fifty-three!'

Chapter Fourteen

The conference next day was in Pacey's own room. It was a much more informal affair than the previous one. The colonel sat on the edge of the superintendent's desk, smoking a small cheroot, while Leighton Powell, Meadows, Rees and Pacey sat or stood wherever they could amongst the cramped furniture of the small room.

'So we still know that the body is that of a five foot four young woman, anyway. This damned bombshell hasn't altered any of the medical evidence, I hope?'

The colonel's usual suave manner had been rubbed a little thin by the panic to find a new approach to solving the identity of the Tremabon skeleton now made famous by Peter Adams' front page article in that morning's *News*.

'It's added to the medical knowledge, actually,' contradicted the pathologist gently.

Barton jerked the cigar out of his mouth. 'Added to it? How the devil can it do that?'

'Before this, we thought that she was a red-headed woman. Now I'm quite certain she isn't.'

It was Pacey's turn to look astonished.

'Why not? That red hair was quite genuine, according to the lab.'

'Genuine all right – and cut at both ends. If our murderer was smart enough to fool us into thinking that the body was thirty years old, instead of less than nine, I'll bet my bottom dollar that the red hair doesn't belong to her. He would have cut off all her own hair down to the scalp and slung in some auburn, just to confuse us. So now we can be quite sure that the original owner was blonde or brunette – otherwise, there would be no point in changing it.'

Pacey breathed heavily. 'Fine! All we have to do now is to find a five foot four blonde, or brunette, missing from somewhere in Great Britain between nineteen fifty-three and about nineteen sixty!'

The colonel stared at the glowing tip of his cheroot.

'Professor, there's no doubt that this Terylene gag is consistent with your estimate of the time of death? I mean, this can still be a burial within the last few years, as far as you are concerned?'

'Yes, there's no trouble there. If you remember, I said anything from two to two hundred years, so give me credit for that!'

Pacey slumped into a chair in the corner of the untidy office.

'How did your people in the lab come to spot this thread?' he asked Meadows.

'During a routine examination of the stuff, one of the boys found that a certain button didn't fall off the cloth when it was touched, as the others did. His inquiring mind wanted to know why and discovering that it was a non-rotting synthetic fibre was easy after that. They've got ways of telling Terylene from nylon and other man-made threads.'

Powell turned his head back to where Pacey was sitting.

'How did young Adams get hold of these X-rays that you sent down to me last night?'

'I didn't bother to ask details – I was too shattered by this other news,' the superintendent replied ruefully. 'But I gather that he went up to Liverpool and tracked down an old sinus operation that the real Mavis had done years ago.

Powell smote his forehead with his fist. 'My God! That's something that never occurred to me.'

'Well, sir, it was hardly likely to unless you knew of it.

If it's anyone's fault, it's mine for not squeezing every drop of information out of old Hewitt.'

The chief constable looked a little severe. 'This thread and button business is quite fortunate, in a way,' he said heavily. 'It saves us from being made to look complete fools by those X-rays, if they were genuine.'

'I've got no doubts that they are the real thing,' said Leighton Powell. 'The films are certainly antique and the skull shows a definite sinus disease. But what's more important is that they look nothing at all like the skull from Tremabon.'

There was a momentary lull in the discussion as each one brooded on the way that some unknown killer had kept them fooled.

The colonel kicked off again, after a moment.

'So what's your next move, Mr Pacey?'

The detective crooked a finger at Willie Rees, who was skulking in a corner of the room.

'Inspector Rees here has spent a fortune of the ratepayers' money on phone calls to various police headquarters to get lists of their missing persons. I only wish there was a central bureau for the whole country, like they have in the London area. It would save all this mucking about with lots of little districts.'

Rees cleared his throat. He was always a little wary of the chief constable, who reminded him far too strongly of his wartime company commander. 'I limited the area a lot, sir. I got details of women missing from Wales, Liverpool, Bristol and the West Midlands.'

'Casting your net a bit wide, weren't you?' said Barton.

'We may have to go a lot further yet,' growled Pacey. 'If nothing comes of that lot, we'll do the rest of the Midlands and then London.'

Meadows diffidently broke into the discussion. 'But, surely, only a local man would know of that particular shaft, facing out to sea and all that?'

'And the existence of the Mavis Hewitt legend,' added Powell.

Pacey wagged his head patiently. 'Agreed. But the girl needn't be a local as well – in fact, it seems certain that she isn't. Rees says that there's no one missing during these years from this county, or any of the adjoining ones, who could possibly fit the bill.'

'How the hell did she get there, then?' demanded Barton.

Pacey heaved his big shoulders. 'That's what I hope to find out, sir – one day!'

Willie Rees looked hesitantly from one to the other, then carried on with his explanation. 'That was the area I took, anyway. Then I limited the requests to women between the ages of twenty-two and thirty-five, just to be on the safe side.'

'You didn't specify any range of height – say, under five foot five?' asked the colonel.

'No, sir. I thought that as there had already been such a lot of mucking about with clothes and hair, there might be something fishy about the height, so I asked for them all.'

'Huh, I don't see how he could shorten her legs – but carry on.'

Willie, becoming more harassed than ever from his chief's nagging, stumbled on with his story.

'I limited the years to fifty-three to sixty. The professor had said that the remains couldn't be less than two years old.'

Powell blew his nose violently. 'I've given up being surprised at anything in this game, but I'll stick my neck out that far.'

'Well, sir, that brought me in thirty-six names for the list. I've got the copies of their descriptions here, and I've managed to go through them all just the once, so far.' Rees held out a sheaf of typewritten papers.

The colonel ground his cigar butt into Pacey's ashtray.

'Thirty-six! I hope you're going to whittle that lot down a bit.'

'I've already cut it to a short list of sixteen, sir.'

The lanky detective consulted another piece of paper.

'Eighteen were eliminated on height – for the first run-through, anyway. I took an inch on either side of five foot four, as the professor said, and scrubbed all those outside that limit.'

Powell looked slightly uncomfortable. 'You've got a touching faith in science, Inspector,' he said with a smile. 'I think that should be all right. But if you get an otherwise dead cert who is half an inch too big or too small, I would keep her in mind, all the same.'

Pacey summarized his assistant's work. 'So you've got another eighteen with nothing to choose between them, Rees?'

'Yes. But that's in the area I chose, mind.'

'Can we narrow those down to even less? It would save us a devil of a lot of chasing around the countryside.' Rees looked hopefully at Powell, who seemed to be meditating.

'Any with red hair among them?' asked the pathologist. Rees had the answer off pat, without looking at his list. 'Yes, four of them, Doctor.'

'Well, that's another four excluded, on my theory.'

'Wait a moment,' cut in Pacey. 'We can't do that.'

'Why not?'

'I'll bet a couple of those were dyed auburn - our murderer is too clever a bloke not to have thought of that one. Real red hair would be just as effective a fake against dyed red hair as against a blonde. The real Mavis was a genuine auburn.'

There was silence again as the others worked out the rather tangled reasoning of this one.

'Any advance on eighteen?' asked Pacey.

'Of course!' The pathologist suddenly smashed his fist into his other palm in a gesture of inspiration. 'The teeth –

at last, I've got a chance to show off with those. If we can get as many dental records as possible of all these girls, I can eliminate most of your list. In fact, if our girl is amongst them, I might even be able to pinpoint her for you!'

Everyone shifted their position, to stare expectantly at the professor. The chief constable put all their thoughts into words. 'That sounds almost too good to be true. How could you possibly do it?'

Leighton reached for a spare piece of paper from the desk and produced a pencil.

'I'll show you,' he said, rapidly sketching two semicircles on the paper. 'These are the upper and lower jaws of our skull.' He drew five small rings at various places on the semicircles. 'These represent the five teeth which are missing from the skull. The sockets are quite normal, so that means one of three possibilities: *one*, the teeth dropped out after death – but you didn't find them in your sieves. Or, *two*, they were extracted within a few weeks before death – which is highly unlikely, as there's no disease at all in the other teeth. Or *three*, they were deliberately pulled out after death by the murderer. And that's what I think happened.'

There was an uncomprehending look on every face except that of the speaker.

'What's all this leading up to, sir?' asked Pacey.

'Look, if the killer wants to pass off the body as Mavis, he has to eliminate anything that can be shown to belong to someone else. Now, he hasn't a clue what Mavis's teeth were like, but he guesses – quite correctly – that we won't either. People didn't go so regularly to the dentist in those days. And the record card, even if she did, would hardly survive all these years. But now he has a body, which otherwise is a good match for Mavis, but which has five teeth with fillings. So all he can do is to pull them out and chuck them away!'

The chief constable shuddered at Powell's enthusiasm over the prospect of a killer cracking out his dead victim's teeth.

'With due respect, Doctor, I find that hard to believe. For a start, if there were no records of Mavis's teeth, why didn't he just leave them in his other body?'

'Because fillings date almost as well as clothes. A dentist could have told almost at sight that they were modern fillings, not thirty years old. You see, the techniques and material used would be unmistakeable to an expert.'

Pacey bobbed his head slowly. 'I'm with you now, Professor. But how are you going to apply this to the missing girls list?'

'We get as many dental record cards as we can,' explained Powell. 'Any woman who had even one tooth extracted is out – there wasn't a single dead socket in that skull.'

'How can you tell that?' asked the colonel.

'When a tooth is pulled out during life, the socket gradually collapses and fills up with bone. This starts soon after the extraction and it's obvious after a few weeks.'

Barton seemed to be convinced and the doctor went on talking:

'Then we narrow them down further by scrubbing out all those with fillings in their teeth in any place other than these five.' He tapped his sketch with a finger.

The others nodded their understanding.

'Now, if we came across a woman who had perfect teeth apart from fillings in these same five, and who had had no extractions, on purely statistical grounds, I'd recommend you to be very interested in her as a candidate for our bones.'

Pacey found some objections to this brainwave.

'Two snags, Professor. The first is that I'll bet that we won't be able to find half the dental records – a lot of the women may never have had any to find. The other thing is that, as this killer seems such a cunning bastard, what's to stop him taking out a couple of extra teeth, healthy ones, just to confuse the issue?'

Powell shrugged and grinned wryly. 'Ah, there you have me, Superintendent. Though I think that these days, most people in this age group would have had some dental treatment and so there'd be a record. But, in any case, this is a method to exclude a lot of your list. It will be the ones with no record – unless you find the jackpot one with the five teeth. Yes, it will be the blank cases that will need following up.'

The colonel came in to defend Powell. 'I think it sounds admirable. It will narrow down your list a devil of a lot, Pacey; you should be very thankful for that.'

He changed the subject, turning to speak to Willie Rees.

'Rees, which of these women is nearest to Tremabon?'

'There's one in Swansea, sir. And another in Brecon. The other two are from Cardiff. Those are the only four from Wales.'

Powell looked mildly astonished. 'I'm always amazed at the number of people that just vanish. Where do they get to – they can't all be murdered, or white-slaved!'

'A lot of them take damn good care not to be found,' replied Pacey. 'They either elope, or run away with the lodger. They don't really disappear at all – that is to say, they just change their way of life and keep well clear of their families.'

The chief constable slid off the desk and made for the door.

'You'll get straight on with the job of tracing those dental records, I suppose, Mr Pacey.'

His words were more of a statement than a question.

'Yes, Colonel, right away,' Pacey replied evenly, keeping the exasperation out of his voice. 'I'll get them down to Professor Powell as fast as they come in.'

The chief vanished and Powell and Meadows soon followed, leaving the resident detectives to have a smoke and a cup of tea.

Pacey hoisted his great legs onto his desk and watched the smoke from his cigarette swirl about in the draughty air.

'Willie,' he said after a while. 'Did anything strike you about that last session in here?'

Rees stared at him. 'No, not particularly – what d'you mean?'

'All that guff about skulls and X-rays and teeth and hair – all medical, Willie – all medical.'

The inspector still looked blankly at Pacey.

'Willie, if you had just croaked somebody and had to get rid of the body – would you think to pull out certain teeth, and of the type of fillings and the colour of the hair?'

Rees, still not seeing what the other was getting at, shook his head.

'No, Willie, nor would I. Nor would the majority of lay people.'

'What do you mean by "lay" people?' asked the inspector.

Pacey slid his legs off the desk and crashed them down on to the floor.

'I mean, Willie, that this whole affair smells very "medical" to me. I'm going over to the county reference library for a few minutes. I feel a "hunch" coming over me!' He clumped out, leaving a thoughtful and somewhat mystified Rees sitting in his room.

163

Chapter Fifteen

'I still think we're barking up the wrong tree,' objected Willie Rees.

He and Pacey were striding across the wide road alongside the castle which led to Cardiff Law Courts and Police Headquarters. Two days after the meeting in Cardigan, they had sifted all the information from the list of missing persons and had got down to a shortlist of four.

'But why are you so mad keen on this one?' persisted Rees.

'Because it's the only one to make any sense,' replied the superintendent. 'Look, we had sixteen to chase up at the beginning. Then Powell's scheme about the teeth whittled that down to seven. Right?'

'Yes, thank God – and the professor.'

Pacey did some of his favourite finger-jabbing into Willie's ribs as they neared the elegant civic buildings.

'Seven. Then you found that one of them had a short "polio" leg – so we're down to six.'

The inspector grunted his agreement.

'Then two of the others had photographs available – which any fool could see were impossible to fit on to the professor's skull picture. So they were knocked out and we're stuck with the last four.'

'But I still don't see why you're so sold on the Cardiff girl. That other one from Bristol seemed a dead ringer to me. And we had a photo of her which fitted the skull like a glove.'

'This one might, if we can get a picture.'

'Might – and it might not!'

'Well, I've got my money on this one, Willie. I feel it in my bones. I'll lay you a dollar that it won't turn out to be the one from Bristol. There now!'

Rees scowled again. 'I'm not taking you; you've screwed too many dollars out of me like that in the past,' he grumbled. 'I reckon you've got something up your sleeve that the rest of us don't know about.'

Pacey was all wide-eyed innocence. 'What, me? I wouldn't hold out on you. Now, would I, Willie?'

The inspector's unprintable reply coincided with their arrival at the police headquarters, much to the disgust of a policewoman standing on the steps.

Within a few minutes, they were shown into a room where a swarthy police officer in plain clothes sat at a table. After introducing himself as Detective Inspector Austin, he waved them to a couple of seats and told them what he had to offer.

'We've had one missing girl on the books for seven years,' he started. 'We haven't been very interested until now – as she was one of the "fly-by-night" type, if you get me.'

Pacey eyed him with professional interest and decided that, although the Cardiff man was cocky-looking and wore far too natty a suit, he was very much on the ball. Austin picked up a record card from the table.

'Julie Gordon, her name was. In November, fifty-five, another woman called Edna Collins reported her missing. She shared a flat with Gordon. They both worked as hostess-cum-barmaids at a posh drinking club in town. This Collins said that the girl Gordon had been in the club as usual on the Friday night, but hadn't shown up since. She reported it on the following Wednesday, by the way. Apparently, it wasn't all that unusual for Julie to buzz off for the odd weekend – presumably dirty – but she'd never stayed away as long as this before. And, by the time the middle of the week came without any sign of her, the room-mate thought she had better tell somebody.'

The detective paused, turned over the card and then flipped it back again.

'And that's about all. We went through the usual routine – inquiries at the club, circulating the description and notifying the Bureau, but we've never heard a word since then about her. At least, not until you telephoned yesterday with a description that fits this one, for what it's worth.'

Pacey looked across the table with interest in his face. 'What about relatives?''

'A dead loss – the girl was originally from an orphanage, according to this Collins. She came from London, via Birmingham, where she had the same sort of background – barmaid, theatre usherette, club hostess. No record of being a "tom", you understand, but it sounds as if she was pretty accommodating to the club members and anyone else in trousers who took her fancy. This Collins character is of the same sort.'

Pacey's fingers tapped the edge of his chair as he listened.

'What about her appearance – hair and all that?'

The local man's eyes dropped back to the card. 'Five foot four, as you said it had to be over the phone; black hair; "good-looking" – I don't know whose opinion that was, but there's a photo here that the other woman gave us. Only a small one, but she certainly looks a dish in it!' He gazed at the snap with relish.

'You were telling me about the hair,' said Pacey, dragging the other man's attention away from the picture.

'Ah, yes – Collins said it was jet black, but she used to have it dyed. The real colour was mousey brown.' He handed the photograph and a negative over to Pacey. 'As you can see, she was ash blonde when this was taken.'

'What else do we know about her?'

'Collins said that she never remembers her going to a

167

dentist since she came to Cardiff, but that Julie had some fillings in her teeth. She's no idea which ones, of course.'

'What about this Collins?' asked Pacey. 'Are her present whereabouts known at all?'

The Cardiff detective smiled smugly. 'She's still in the same job, in the same bar. She's got a smart little flat in the centre of town. The boys on the beat say they've had their eye on her place from time to time, but nothing definite is known about what she uses it for. I've heard a squeak myself that the club owner pays the rent.'

Pacey looked slightly pained at this recital of the seamier side of life in his capital city.

''Yes, that's fine. But can we get out to see her this afternoon, d'you think? I want to call in Swansea on the way back, if there's time.'

Austin's grin got broader and even more self-satisfied as he lifted his telephone and spoke into it. 'Send her up, Jim, will you?'

He put the receiver down and kept on looking pleased with himself. 'I arranged for her to come here and meet you. She seems keen to keep on the right side of us, so she's been waiting downstairs for you.'

A tap on the door heralded a uniformed constable, who ushered in the former room-mate of the possibly late Miss Julie Gordon.

Edna Collins was a striking pink-rinsed blonde. Although just beginning to go to seed, she was still attractive in a brassy sort of way.

The eyes of the local detective made a rapid tour of appreciation, and he fumbled with the Windsor knot of his narrow tie as he asked her to sit down. Pacey dragged a chair forward for her and sat back to study her closely from under his shaggy brows.

Over-heavy make-up, over-false lashes and a bold pair of eyes gave her the look of an upper crust barmaid to perfection. She was overdressed, the weather being hardly cold enough for the black topcoat with an enormous white fur collar. She sat down and eyed the three men with the assurance of a woman who knows exactly the impression she makes with the opposite sex.

'It's about Julie, you said?' she began, without any preamble. Her accent was unmistakably that of a Londoner.

'Yes, Miss Collins. These gentlemen are CID officers from West Wales who would like to ask you a few things about her disappearance. I'm sure that you'll be willing to do anything to help us clear up the mystery about your friend.'

'Has she turned up then?' Edna sounded incredulous.

'No, not exactly,' Pacey answered evasively. 'We think she may have been involved in an accident. We want to see if the girl we're interested in could be Miss Gordon.'

'Well, couldn't I just go and see her? I'd soon tell you if it was Julie or not.' The hard voice suited her appearance.

'No, I'm afraid we haven't got her to show you,' said Pacey, somewhat ambiguously. 'We'll have to go about it another way.'

Edna loosened her coat, revealing a prominent bosom, tightly sheathed in a bright red dress.

'I'll do all I can for you, I'm sure.'

Her powdered skin was stretched across her high cheekbones and, for a moment, Pacey was reminded of the skull from the lonely cliff.

'I'd like to hear all about the disappearance again. I know it was a long time ago; over seven years. But I want to know everything that you can remember.'

Edna Collins spun her story out over a few minutes; but it boiled down to no more than the summary that Austin had given them.

'What about the days immediately before she vanished? Anything odd about them, that you can recall?'

The pink head shook in reply. 'No, I can't say there was.'

'What about her friends – any particular ones you know of? Would she have been likely to have gone off with some man – or even got married on the hop?'

Collins threw back her head and laughed.

Not a very attractive laugh, Pacey thought.

'Married?' she exclaimed. 'God no, not Julie. She had too much fun staying single – like me!' She caught the resident inspector's eye and smiled archly at him. 'Anyway, she'd have told me, and I'm damn sure she wouldn't have left all her clothes behind at our place.'

Pacey fixed her with his eyes. 'She left all her things behind, you say?'

'Yes, that's right – and she thought the world of her clothes.'

'Didn't she take anything at all, like a weekend case?'

'No, not a single thing. Just what she was wearing when we closed on the Friday night.'

'It doesn't say anything on the record about you telling us that she left all her stuff behind,' Austin said accusingly.

'Hard luck, darling!' the hostess replied easily. 'Blame your coppers then, because I told them all right.'

Pacey went back to his earlier question. 'Any boyfriends – particular ones?'

'Dozens of them! Everybody was Julie's friend. I always told her she was too easygoing.'

'Yes, but did she have any particular boyfriend around the time she disappeared?'

'Not for more than a week at a time,' grinned the woman.

'Which one was it *that* week?' Pacey asked doggedly.

The garish fur collar jerked as she shrugged.

'It's hard to say – she ran so many at the same time. I remember that there was a chap in the club several nights that week who seemed to be making quite a play for Julie. I remember him because I thought that I wouldn't mind getting to know him myself,' she added reflectively.

'Why – was he good-looking, then?' Pacey asked shortly.

'No, not really. I don't go for the film star type myself,' said Edna, airily, looking pointedly at Austin. 'This chap wasn't ugly, not by any means. But he had character – you know what I mean?'

'Know who he was?' demanded the superintendent.

'Not a clue. He was only around for those few days. I don't think he came in after that Friday. I only remember him at all because I had a passing fancy for him myself. I wondered when Julie didn't come in on the Saturday whether or not she'd gone off for the weekend with him – bit of jealousy, I guess!'

She winked at Austin, who was the most appreciative member of her audience.

'Would you know him again if you saw him?' asked Pacey.

Edna thought for a moment, her reddened lips pursed. 'It was a long time ago, but – yes, I reckon I might recognize him. He was in the bar quite a bit that week, so I had plenty of time to get a good look at him.'

'How would you describe him, then?'

The brassy barmaid pondered this a few seconds. 'Well, I don't know how to put it in words – how do you describe anyone? He wasn't good-looking, as I've said; not a bad face, a bit thin. Brown hair, I think; just ordinary. Average height. He'd be about twenty-five to thirty, I suppose.'

Pacey restrained a groan. This was the standard description of the average man. Apart from the guess at the age, the account she had just given would probably have fitted sixty per cent of the males in Great Britain.

'Did you speak to him?'

'Only in passing, a couple of times. Not for want of trying. But Julie was working hard on him, so she didn't give me much of a chance. I seem to remember that his voice was a bit different, the little I heard of it.'

Her pencilled brows came closer together as she made an effort to remember.

'What do you mean – "different"?' asked Pacey.

'He certainly wasn't a local. I can't place what he sounded like now, but I've got an idea in the back of my mind that he might have been a German.'

'A *German*!' exclaimed Pacey, looking across at Willie in disgust.

'Only an idea, that is. I can't really remember,' the woman said coldly. 'I can't trot out the descriptions of all the men that come into the club. There are thousands of them in a year.'

'How did you manage to remember this one then?' Pacey demanded suspiciously.

'Don't suppose I would have, only he seemed to be the current heart-throb at the time Julie pushed off. I wondered whether she'd hopped it for a weekend with him, as I've already said.'

'I still don't see why you didn't tell the police about her things left behind in the flat, and about this man,' complained the Cardiff detective.

'I probably did, and your bobbies forgot to put it down in their little books!' Edna countered sarcastically.

Pacey broke in on the developing wrangle.

'Thank you very much for your help, Miss Collins. There's something else you could do for us which might help a lot to clear up the mystery about your friend.'

'What's that?' she asked suspiciously.

'I'd like you to take a trip down to West Wales and see if you can identify the man you saw with Julie Gordon during the week before she vanished.'

The blonde's eyes widened. 'West Wales! Where there,

for Pete's sake?'

'Aberystwyth.'

Either she never read the newspapers or her geography was very poor, for she failed to associate the place with the recently notorious Tremabon.

'That's a devil of a long way,' she complained. 'When d'you want to drag me all the way down there?'

'I'm not quite sure – probably within the next few days. We'll let you know in plenty of time. And, of course, you'll get your travelling expenses and a good allowance for your time and trouble.'

The woman looked doubtful, but the novelty of the idea began to play on her sense of importance.

'Well, if you can fix it with Henry – that's my employer – I suppose it's all right with me.'

A few more minutes settled the details and the blonde swayed her way out of the room.

Pacey stood up, ready to leave.

'Thanks a lot for your help,' he said to Austin. 'We may need some more of it in a day or so, but I'll have to go back home and do some more spadework first.

The smooth inspector saw them out with a promise to give them any more assistance that they needed. The Cardiganshire men walked briskly back to their waiting car and set off for home.

'We'll stop off at Swansea on the way back, Willie. I want to ask the professor a few questions.' He gave some directions to the driver and settled back in his seat.

'Pardon me for asking,' said Rees with heavy sarcasm. 'But what the hell is going on? What are we rushing back to do this time?'

As they sped along the A48, Pacey relented and unloaded his hunch on to Willie Rees.

'I told you a couple of days ago that I thought this affair reeked of medicine, so to speak. So, just for the hell

173

of it, I set to wondering what doctor could possibly be involved.'

'There's only the Ellis-Morgans in Tremabon,' objected Rees.

'Yes. Three of 'em! That's enough for a start. Now, any one of them could have both the medical know-how, and the local knowledge that this case is stiff with.'

'Sounds bloody daft to me!' grumbled his assistant.

'Look, just string along with me, Willie,' pleaded Pacey. 'Just think of it as a mental exercise, eh? Now, which one of the three would you put your money on?'

'None of them,' the inspector replied promptly.

Pacey sighed. 'All right. Well, which one would you say is the most unlikely to be involved?'

'The old one, of course. I can't see him knocking off a young bird like this ... even if it is her – which I doubt very much. I still fancy the Bristol dame.'

'OK, so it's one of the younger Ellis-Morgans. Which one?'

'I don't know,' said Rees, irritably. 'The whole idea is barmy. I'd never met any of them until a couple of days ago, so how would I know which one is a homicidal maniac?'

His sarcasm was wasted on the thick skin of the superintendent.

'I didn't know anything about them, either, until the day before yesterday, when I went to the public library.'

'What's that got to do with it?'

'I looked them up in the Medical Directory. The old man qualified in nineteen twenty-five and has been in Tremabon since thirty-one. Gerald qualified in London in fifty-three. He did a year there as house surgeon, then came to work with his father. David passed out in Cardiff in fifty-two and did three years pathology there after finishing his house-jobs. That means he lived in Cardiff until fifty-six. Then he packed up pathology and came home to work with his dad.'

Willie looked suspiciously at Pacey. 'So what? Just because a bloke lived in Cardiff for a few years, that doesn't make him a flaming murderer, does it?'

'I agree, but we've got to start somewhere. And this seems as good a place as any.'

'And is that the only reason why you're more interested in the Cardiff girl than the Bristol one – because that doctor lived here until fifty-six?' Rees asked incredulously. He had a sudden longing for the corpse to be the girl from Bristol, merely to be able to crow over the fat man sitting alongside him.

'That's it,' Pacey replied calmly. 'Now that we've started, we may as well follow it to the bitter end before handing in our cards.'

'What do you mean by that?'

'Our dear chief constable – bless him! – is letting us work out this first bunch of missing persons. And, if nothing comes of them, he's handing the case over to the Yard.'

'And the best of British luck to them!' growled Rees. Both of them sat thinking for a moment, each knowing what was in the other's mind. The county forces were still reluctant to give up their big cases to the Central Office; they thought, sometimes with justification, that they could handle them just as well themselves. The Yard's main advantage was in obtaining the co-operation of *all* forces when widespread inquiries were needed – as some county constabularies seemed to engage in private vendettas with each other.

'So what do we do next?' asked Willie Rees.

'Just for fun, let's say David Ellis-Morgan clobbered this girl Gordon in Cardiff back in fifty-five. What should we look for now?'

'Hell of a long time ago! If he tried to cut her arm off, there might have been bloodstains around somewhere, I suppose.'

Rees grudgingly allowed himself to humour Pacey by playing his game of make-believe with him.

'Where would *you* look, Willie?'

'In his house, or wherever he did her in.'

Pacey grinned. 'Do you think he carried her the eighty-odd miles from Cardiff to Tremabon on his back?'

'Oh, a car. Yes, but he won't have the same one now, will he?'

'"No, but you're going to start looking for it this afternoon, boy. And, when you find it, you're going to get the forensic chaps to go over every square inch of it for blood.'

'After seven years' hard wear?' countered Rees in an offended voice.

'Why not? I read the other day that they even grouped the blood of an Egyptian mummy after three thousand years, so I don't see why seven should strain them too much.'

'And that's my first job, is it?'

'Your *only* one for the time being. I've already asked the Cardiff CID to find out where Ellis-Morgan was living, and to see if they can get a good look at the premises.'

Rees sat stonily for a moment. 'You know, Super, this is all very well,' he said eventually; 'but aren't we mucking about wasting time? I'll admit that I think your theory is all a lot of tripe. But the quickest way to kill it would surely be to let that Collins woman have a look at the doctor. Her "yes" or "no" would be the finish of it, near enough – especially as I'm damn sure she'll say "no".'

'I'm going to do that – but I want a day or so to try to dig up some corroboration, if that's possible. This attempt at identification will have to be done very tactfully, Willie, to say the least. The colonel would blow a gasket if he thought I was lining up one of the county's most respected

GPs for an identity parade. No, boy, we've got to do this subtly and try to get a bit of extra ammunition up our sleeves for our own protection. That's why I want you to find that car, and why I'm going to call on the pathologist.'

A couple of hours later, they were standing at the door of the post-mortem room in the medical school in Swansea, watching Leighton Powell as he stood cheerfully in his rubber boots and plastic apron amongst half a dozen gutted corpses in the long chilly room.

Organized confusion reigned about him, as three attendants bustled about, clanging enamel trays full of organs and noisily dropping instruments into the sinks.

Pacey stood for a few minutes before attracting the attention of the professor, hypnotized by the macabre scene lit by the harsh fluorescent lights. For all his years of familiarity with violence and sudden death, the sight of the wholesale carnage in a public mortuary still gave him a momentary heave of the stomach.

Powell caught sight of the two detectives and hurried across to them, pulling off his rubber gloves. He hustled them into a side office and took off his gown and apron.

'I'm sorry to interrupt you, sir,' began Pacey. 'But we've raised another possible candidate for the Tremabon bones and I'd like to know what you think of it from your angle.'

Powell struggled with his Wellington boots. 'Of course. Let me get these togs off, and I'll take you up to my rooms, away from this blasted smell!'

A few minutes later, Pacey was showing the doctor the photograph of the club girl from Cardiff.

'This is Julie Gordon, a sort of high-class barmaid. She upped and vanished in fifty-five.'

The professor studied the photograph. It was a copy of a picture of professional quality and showed the face and shoulders of an attractive girl, with a saucy pair of eyes and a full-lipped mouth.

'Very nice, too,' he said appreciatively. 'But what about this hair? It looks a false blonde, if I ever saw one.'

Pacey explained, 'It was bleached, when the photo was taken. But her pal, who reported her missing, said that it was dyed black at the time she vanished. The real colour was mousey-brown, apparently.'

'And her age and size?'

'Twenty-seven and five foot four. There's no record of dental work; they couldn't trace her before she came to Cardiff, but she had some teeth filled. I don't know which ones.'

'What exactly do you want me to tell you, Mr Pacey?'

'I just want you to check that there's nothing in the facts that we have about Julie Gordon here, such as they are, that would rule her out as a candidate for the Tremabon skeleton.'

Powell looked quizzically at the superintendent.

'Have you got anyone on the hook, then?'

Pacey grinned evasively. 'I'm thinking of sticking my neck out if you give me the OK, Professor. Sticking it out so far that I daren't tell even you what I suspect until I get a bit of confirmation.'

Powell respected Pacey's reluctance to let the cat out of his bag, so didn't press him any further.

'I can't help you an awful lot, I'm afraid,' he said. 'The age is right, the height is right and, as we know nothing about the teeth, that doesn't help one way or the other. The only other thing I can do is to check the skull against this photo here. After the Mavis Hewitt fiasco, though, I've got even less faith in that method than I had before.'

'I'd like you to do it, if you would, sir,' asked Pacey. 'I'll have to get this photo copied up to size, then.' Pacey fished in his breast pocket. 'If it would save time, I've got the negative of that photo here. The Cardiff police copied the original and loaned me the negative as well.' Powell took the square of black celluloid and held it up to the window.

'Well, it's almost exactly full-face, so I could do a very rough check here and now. It'd not be at all accurate; but it ought to show up any glaring failure to correspond.'

He turned to a side bench and began fiddling with a slide projector and a large picture of the Tremabon skull which was mounted on a sheet of cardboard.

Willie Rees took the opportunity, while the doctor was busy, of looking around and satisfying his curiosity about the inside of a forensic pathologist's den.

If he expected glass jars full of mutilated organs and rows of grinning skulls on the shelves, he must have been very disappointed.

The main feature of the room was paper.

There were stacks of white forms, piles of large blue forms, and heaps of tattered flimsies. A generous drift of quarto typescript lay like snow on all the available desk and bench space and even overflowed onto the floor. There were bookcases full of books and untidy rows of box files peeped through the avalanche of paper.

A small sink was embedded in the bench below the window and contained several empty bottles, a dirty cup and saucer, and a potted plant.

Rees' now despairing eye, nurtured by newspaper articles about Spilsbury and his colleagues, was slightly revived by the sight of a gleaming microscope, the dramatic effect of which was spoilt by a postcard propped against the twin eyepieces. On it was scrawled the mundane message – "Remember to buy cabbage on way home"!

On the floor below the sink was a large cardboard box, bearing the emblem of 'Gusto Baked Beans'. Below this, the detective noticed that the words "Mavis Hewitt" had been written in crayon, followed by a large and significant question mark.

Now utterly disillusioned, Willie turned to watch the pathologist as he finished erecting his makeshift apparatus.

'I've put the negative in the projector,' he explained as he switched it on. 'And I'll shine the image of it onto the skull photo, to see how they coincide.'

He closed the slatted sunblind to darken the room and then slid the projector back and forth along the benchtop until the face on the negative was the same size as the skull.

'There we are – not bad, is it, for a rough check?'

Powell moved the cardboard of the skull photograph around until it coincided exactly with the rays from the projector. Pacey and Willie Rees crowded behind him and craned their neck to squint down the line of the bench.

'Looks just as good as the Mavis Hewitt one,' said Pacey in a self-satisfied tone. 'Same size jaw and eye sockets.'

The professor grimaced into the darkened room. 'And it might be just as much of a red herring, too. Still, there's nothing here to justify me telling you that you're wasting your time with this girl. The front teeth – what little of them show – are the same shape, the width of the cheekbones are the same and the eye sockets are the same shape, and distance apart.' He dropped the card and went to open the sunblinds.

'And that's about all I can tell you, I'm afraid.'

Pacey looked satisfied at even this most cautious of opinions.

'There is one more thing, sir. This woman was reported missing in nineteen fifty-five. Is that all right as far as your date of death is concerned?'

Powell grinned. 'I seem to get asked this question about twice a day! Yes, Superintendent, I know it's being wise after the event, but I've said all along that anything more than two or three years will satisfy me. If this one here is the true bill, I'll admit that I'm a bit surprised that the soft tissue on the bones being so far gone in seven years. Even the membrane around the shaft of the bone, and the last traces of gristle around the joints, have gone.'

Pacey looked a bit upset at this. 'But you're not going to rule out seven years as being possible, are you?'

'No, no. I'd be a fool to say it couldn't happen. Almost anything can happen in this game. That's why it's so foolish to be dogmatic. As I told you before, I've seen a body reduced to skeleton in less than a year; but then the bones still had tags of fibre and gristle on them. But seven years is a dickens of a lot longer, isn't it? And that mine was very damp and not far below the surface – the ground water, which must have been heavily contaminated by sheep, is certain to have been seeping over the body all the time. No, I won't quibble about seven years. If you can find your other evidence to pin the identity on this girl, I'll back you up all the way with the medical guff.'

There was nothing more that Pacey could learn from the professor. Soon he and Rees made their way back to Cardigan, leaving the elusive 'Miss X' quietly resting in her baked bean carton under Powell's bench.

Chapter Sixteen

On the following morning, the Tuesday of the week after the skeleton was first discovered, Pacey and Rees managed to get down to the backlog of work on other cases for a few hours.

Willie had contrived to swing Pacey's order to find Ellis-Morgan's old car on to Detective Sergeant Mostyn, while he himself dealt with the welter of paper in his 'In' tray.

About mid-morning, he went into Pacey's office to have a chat over their 'cuppa and a fag' – an established part of the CID routine.

The burly superintendent was relaxing in his favourite posture, his collar button open, coat off and large boots up on his desk.

'Willie,' he said, after important matters like last night's television and the rugby prospects for the weekend had been dealt with. 'Willie, did that fancy DI in Cardiff say anything to you about finding the place where David Ellis-Morgan lived when he was a doctor up there?'

Rees shook his head. 'No, why should he?'

'I asked him on the phone on Saturday if he could have a snoop around. He obviously hasn't had any joy yet. What about Mostyn? You sent him out to look for that car, did you?'

Willie grinned sheepishly. 'Yes, 'fraid so. If the doctor sold it to a Scotsman, he might be in Glasgow by now!'

'You're a real scream, Willie,' Pacey said coldly. 'More likely the ruddy thing has been melted down for scrap by now.'

In actual fact, Mostyn had struck lucky and, by lunchtime, was looking at the car that had once belonged to the doctor. He had expected the tracking down process to be long and tedious, especially as he had to use the discretion impressed on him by Pacey. However, from the time when he had arrived at the police house in Tremabon, everything had been made easy for him. He had learned from the local PC that the doctor had only possessed two cars, still having the second one at the moment.

'He bought his first one, a Ford estate car, when he was in Cardiff,' said Griffith, mystified by the query. 'He used it right up to a couple of years ago, when he bought his Austin-Healey.'

'Any idea what the registration number was?' the sergeant asked hopefully. 'I could trace it through the county registration people then, as I can't ask him personally.'

Griffith grinned at him. 'I can't remember the number, no – but if it's just finding the car that you want, I can tell you where it is.'

Mostyn almost fell on the constable's neck with gratitude.

'Where is it? Somebody local bought it, did they?'

'Dr David traded it in for his new car in Aberystwyth. Harry Sayers, the garage owner, uses it in the business – for running around with spares and that sort of thing.'

Mostyn drove to the seaside town and found the garage. He noticed an old Zephyr station wagon parked outside and the owner confirmed that this was the vehicle in question. To cover the delicate situation, Mostyn had to pitch him a fictitious story.

'This is in strict confidence, Mr Sayers, but we need to have the car for examination by our laboratory – only until tomorrow morning.'

The other man looked anxious. 'Nothing *I've* done, I hope?'

'No, it's to do with something that happened when the previous owner had it. It may have been involved in an accident with another vehicle and a serious charge is pending – on the other driver, of course. We want to make some paint tests and other examinations, that's all.'

The sergeant managed to blind the other with a bit of science and got his permission to borrow the Ford until the next day. He had a driver in the police car, who took it back to Cardigan while he drove the Ford himself. He parked it in the headquarters yard and arranged for the forensic experts to come up early next morning to go over it for bloodstains.

He was back in Pacey's office in time to be grabbed by the superintendent and hustled back out through the door.

'We're going to Cardiff, me boy. Willie, hold the fort and carry on with all that "bumf" – I'll be back later on today, with a bit of luck,' he called over his shoulder as he poked the protesting Mostyn in front of him, his usual aloof manner punctured by indignation.

'I've only just this minute got back with that car of the doctor's. I haven't even had any lunch yet. Where have I got to go now?'

'We can have a bite to eat on the way. I'll tell you all about it then.'

Over a pint and a cheese roll in a roadside public house, Pacey briefly explained the set-up to his sergeant.

'I told you before that we're thinking that this Julie Gordon woman might be our skeleton – and I expect you've gathered that we've got David Ellis-Morgan even more tentatively lined up as a suspect.'

Mostyn nodded. 'Inspector Rees gave me the general idea.'

'Well, in that case, you'll probably know that the doctor spent a few years as a hospital pathologist in

Cardiff – where the missing Julie came from. Well, the Cardiff CID have been hot on the trail for us since I asked them for help. They've got a spiv-type DI there who looks like a barrow boy, but he's hot stuff on getting things done. He's dug up a pal of the missing girl – found that she has had a blood group done at some time. And, now, he's tracked down the flat where Ellis-Morgan lived when he was working there.'

'What help is that to us?'

'The resident pathologist, so this DI told me on the phone just now, used to live in a flat in a house near the hospital. The place hasn't been used for living in for a few years now, so this Cardiff rozzer – Austin, his name is – went snooping around there yesterday. I don't know what yarn he spun to the hospital authorities, but he got in and had a good look around. In the old bathroom, he found some stains on the floorboards under a join in the lino. He took a scraping to the Cardiff forensic lab – and it turned out to be good honest blood!'

Mostyn had his doubting Thomas expression fixed well into position. 'That doesn't mean much – perhaps someone had been cutting their toenails too close after a bath.'

'Maybe. But it's worth a trip to see for ourselves.'

'Was it human blood?'

'We don't know that either, yet. But I can't see what other sort it's likely to be in a bathroom – as the days of illegal pig-slaughtering are over. The Swansea lab is going to handle that part of it, as the only possible connection is with our case. Meadows is going to meet us at this flat.'

It turned out to be the whole attic floor of four rooms in an old house immediately opposite the hospital. The ground floor was still used as a fracture clinic; the first floor was a dumping ground for discarded hospital equipment; and the flat itself was half full of old record cards and patients' case notes.

The ever-keen Inspector Austin, wearing a too-blue suit

and a hand-painted tie was waiting with Meadows in the bathroom. A police photographer, with a tripod and a resigned expression, was leaning against the passage wall outside.

'I've pulled the lino right up,' said Austin. 'You can see the stains. I've had them photographed already.'

Pacey and Mostyn looked into the small room and stared at the floor.

A double line of tin-tacks showed where the linoleum had been fixed across the centre of the room. Between the lines, level with the centre of the bath, was a brown stain. It stretched between the tacks for six inches, running along the middle of a board. Then it spread out into a dappled circle, the edges of which vanished down the cracks between the adjoining planks.

'That's where I took a splinter out with a knife,' said Austin, pointing at a fresh scar in the wood. 'Real one hundred per cent blood!'

Meadows dropped to his knees and looked closely at the stain.

'Quite old, that's for sure. I'd better prise up the whole plank. There's a join in it halfway, thank the Lord!' He produced a long, flat chisel and with a couple of strong wrenches and a squeal of tortured nails, had the six foot board out in a moment.

'What are the hospital people going to say about this?' asked Pacey, as he watched Meadows slip a large plastic bag over each end of the plank.

'They can say what they bloody well like. I'll square the secretary with some yarn for the time being,' said the local detective.

Pacey bent down and looked into the dusty hole left by the removal of the floorboard.

'No stains or anything else in here. What else can you do for us, Meadows?'

The liaison officer looked carefully around the room.

'Inspector Austin says he's looked at all the other rooms. At least as well as he could with all these bundles of paper lying around. If there's nothing there, the only other hope is that bath.'

Pacey looked at the grimy enamel doubtfully.

'You'd never get anything from the sides of that, surely? Even if it did have blood in it, it would have been washed and wiped a hundred times since then.'

'The bath itself, yes ... but I'm wondering about the waste pipe and the trap underneath. It doesn't look as if it's been removed since nineteen fifty-five.'

Pacey turned to Austin.

'Do you know anything about the history of this place?'

'Ellis-Morgan lived here from fifty-three to fifty-six. Then his successor, a Dr Jones, came. He was only here for about eight months before they closed the flat up. The house is supposed to be demolished to make way for an extension to the hospital. They just use it as a store for the time being.'

Pacey thought for a moment, then spoke to Meadows.

'Will your lab be able to give me any idea how old these stains are?'

'No, not a hope. We can tell you if they're human and probably let you know the main blood groups, that's all.'

The hefty policeman made up his mind and slapped the side of the bath.

'OK, let's have the waste pipe off, then. God knows what the hospital will think. I hope you can fix them, Austin. If any whisper of this gets to the Press, my chief constable will give *me* the Death by a Thousand Cuts!'

'How are we going to get it off?' demanded Meadows, 'Can we get a fitter from the hospital?'

Pacey looked as if his trousers had suddenly been filled with soldier ants. 'Flames, no! Let's keep this to ourselves as much as we can.'

With the aid of the tool kit from a police car, they

managed to prise off the bath panel and unscrew the short U-bend from the bath outlet – which Meadows reverently put into one of his endless supply of polythene bags.

Pacey and Mostyn left Inspector Austin to explain to the hospital the loss of floorboard and waste pipe, and made their way back to West Wales, while Meadows took his 'trophies of the chase,' as he called them.

Pacey, Rees and their sergeant spent the next morning at Tremabon, in a fruitless round of inquiries amongst the villagers.

Pacey had little hope of learning anything new; but he thought that he had better go through the motions of asking about any strange young woman who had been noticed in the village within the last few years.

'A flaming waste of time!' he growled on the way back. 'This is a holiday place – dozens of strange folks come here every summer. And, if I know anything about it, our girl came here for the first time when she was stone dead! And probably in the middle of the night, as well.'

That afternoon, Pacey moped about his office, unusually jumpy and short-tempered. Willie Rees diagnosed the signs as those of indecision. He was right. The senior man was uncertain whether to go ahead with his hunch and bring the girl up to identify Ellis-Morgan. The alternatives were either to do nothing at all – but to carry on with the endless job of sifting through more lists of missing persons – or to go to the chief constable and dump the whole lot in his lap, with a recommendation to call in the Yard.

A telephone call from Swansea eventually helped him to make up his mind. It was Meadows, with a report on the bloodstains.

'We've tested the stuff on the bathroom floorboard,' he said. 'It's human all right; no doubt about it. The precipitin tests are good enough to use as pictures in a textbook!'

Although this was what Pacey had expected – *what*

else, he thought, *but a human would ever be in a bathroom*? – the definite evidence prodded him to take a chance on making a fool of himself.

'OK? I'll risk it. I'll get that girl up tomorrow. Anything else to tell me?'

Meadows' voice came tinnily over the line. 'The group of the blood was A. But, as you've no idea what group your girl was, it doesn't help much.'

'No, blast it! If only we had found a blood donor card, or something like that – but that only happens in books, I suppose. What about that bit of pipe?'

Meadows chuckled at the other end. 'I was waiting for you to ask that? Yes, we got a good, strong, positive benzidine test out of the whole length of the pipe – so it is quite probable that a lot of blood passed down it at some time.'

Pacey sat up and his voice showed that his interest was aroused. 'That's worth hearing. Tell me more!'

'Not much more to say,' Meadows answered cautiously, 'We can't even be definite that the reaction is due to blood, as a few other things also give a positive. The confirmation that *this* is human blood is out of the question, of course.'

'And you can't even say if this blood in the pipe is Group A, like that on the floor?'

'No, not a hope. You see, this benzidine test will pick up one part in three million, it's as sensitive as that. So even the fact that we had a strong positive doesn't mean that there was enough blood left to do fancy tests like grouping and human precipitin reactions.'

Pacey was a little crestfallen but was impressed sufficiently by the results to have made up his mind about his future actions. 'Anything come out of the examinations of that Ford estate wagon?' he went on.

'No, sorry. The boys almost tore it apart – had the floor out from the back and tested every square inch. But there wasn't a thing anywhere.'

Rees came in as Pacey was replacing the telephone on its rest. 'That was Meadows, Willie – he rang to say that the pipe from the bath was positive for blood and that the stains on the floor were human – but there was nothing in the Ford.'

Rees hovered around expectantly. 'So what are we going to do now?'

'I'm taking a chance on it, Willie, and getting that blonde tart up here tomorrow. Let's hope that our Doctor Jones didn't really cut his throat shaving in that bathroom. And, if he did, that he wasn't Group A!'

Chapter Seventeen

On the following afternoon they stood waiting anxiously in a first floor room in the police station at Aberystwyth.

'This seems a very weak excuse to get him to come up from Tremabon,' objected Willie Rees.

'Only way I could do it,' answered Pacey, going to the window and looking out anxiously.

The problem had been to get David Ellis-Morgan to the station without raising any embarrassing questions in the quite likely event of Pacey's hunch fizzling out. Eventually, the superintendent had hit on the idea of asking him to sign a completely unnecessary statement to the effect that he was present and helped at the examination of the bones as they were removed from the mine. As Gerald and his father were also involved, Pacey had been obliged to extend the farce to them as well. He had called in at Carmel House that morning, after making sure that the sons were out, collected the father's signature and arranged for the two younger doctors to call in at the police station in the afternoon, having already fixed up for Edna Collins to be there.

'He should have been here by now – I said half past two.' muttered Pacey, looking for the twentieth time at his watch.

Willie Rees went to the window and looked down into the station yard.

'Here he is now. At least, here's a red Austin-Healey. That's sure to be his!'

'Aye, that'll be David – his brother has got a green Rover, as far as I remember.' Pacey hurried to the door.

'I'll see if that girl is lined up for her job.'

He looked out into the corridor. Sitting on a chair outside the room next to theirs was the hostess from Cardiff. She had a uniformed policewoman sitting alongside her for effect and held a woman's magazine ready to camouflage her face. Pacey was glad to see that she was dressed less conspicuously than the last time he saw her.

'That's fine, Miss Collins. Just try to look as if you weren't there! All I want you to do is to have a crafty look at the man as I bring him along to that room, and again when he leaves. We'll only be a couple of minutes. Listen to his voice as well, if you can.'

He went down the stairs to the charge room where he found David Ellis-Morgan inquiring for him.

'Sorry to drag you up here just for this, Doctor, but we're getting all the documents together in this case and we wanted yours and your brother's statements for continuity. It won't take a minute.'

David seemed to be quite incurious. He followed the detective up the stairs and along the corridor where the two women sat. As they passed Edna Collins, Pacey carefully engineered things so that she would have a chance to hear the doctor speak.

'Will your brother be coming along as well?'

'Yes, he said he would. He's got a call on the outskirts of the town, so it'll be quite easy for him to pop in.'

Pacey opened the office door and they went in. Pacey read over the simple statement to him, and David signed it, the whole process taking only a couple of minutes.

Again, on the way out, Pacey started a conversation in the corridor.

'This sort of thing should be right up your street, sir. I heard that you were a pathologist at one time.'

'Yes, but all hospital work; none of this blood-and-thunder forensic stuff. We "straight" pathologists leave all that to the more cranky members of the profession.'

They passed down the stairs and Pacey saw him off on the steps of the police station.

'Mind if I leave my car in your yard for a couple of minutes?' asked David. 'I want to nip across the road and buy some collars and things.'

He strode off down the street, and Pacey almost ran back up the stairs to hear what Edna Collins had to say.

Willie had taken her into the office by the time he got up there.

'Well, what do you think?' he asked, breathing heavily after dashing up the two flights.

The blonde looked blankly at him.

'Sorry, dear – I never saw him before in my life!'

Some minutes later, when the woman had left to catch her train back to Cardiff, Pacey sat dejectedly with Rees in the upstairs office.

'Looks as if we're all washed up, Willie,' he said. 'The old man is sure to give this to the Yard now. I can't say I blame him. And they're welcome to it.'

'What about the other girls on the list? And all the other areas that we haven't covered?'

'You know as well as I do that there's nothing in those. That Bristol girl turned up two years ago – they forgot to notify the Bureau. The others are hardly worth the trouble of chasing. And, as for starting on the North Country and London, well that's just impossible. Let the Yard do it, and the best of luck to 'em!'

Rees picked up the bogus statement from the desk.

'I may as well tear this up, then?'

Pacey shook his head wearily. 'Better hang on to it until the other brother shows up. It'll look more genuine if we can show him that one when he's signing his own.'

Willie leered sadistically at his colleague. 'I should have taken that dollar bet with you, shouldn't I? What about my idea that it might be this other brother – he's a

195

doctor and knows as much about Tremabon as the first one?'

Pacey scowled at him. 'Oh, shut up, will you? Don't kick a man when he's down. I suppose I'll have to pull myself together and go down to Cardigan now to confess to "Dick" Barton.'

There was a rapid knocking on the door.

'Perhaps this is the other brother,' suggested Rees.

'Sounds a bit anxious, just to sign a statement. Come in!' yelled Pacey.

The door opened and the startled face of Edna Collins appeared.

Pacey jumped to his feet. 'What's the trouble? I thought you were in a hurry to catch your train?'

She came into the room, her heavily powdered face even paler than usual.

'I've seen him – the man in the club – the one you're looking for!'

'What the devil d'you mean! You said just now that it wasn't him?'

'No, no – not the one that came in here … another chap! I was just going down the street when a car pulled up and a man got out. He bumped into me and apologized – then I saw who it was!'

'Did he say anything?'

'I … I don't know. I think he started to speak – I know he recognized me. I could see it in his face – but I just ran!'

'Why did you want to run?' snapped Pacey.

Edna Collins had lost all her brazen self-assurance now. She looked frightened and suddenly old.

'When I saw you in Cardiff, I didn't know what all this was about. I talked to some of the other girls – they told me about the skeleton in the cave, it's been in the papers – and you are the man investigating the – the murder. So it all fits, doesn't it? That man who was with Julie – he's the one you want – that's why I ran.'

'Where did he go?' Pacey said urgently, moving towards the door.

'Into a shop, I think. I ran back here and looked around, but he was gone. His car was still parked at the kerb though.'

'What car was it?'

'A big green one – a Rover, I think. It looked the same as my boss's; he's got a Rover.'

Willie Rees' sparse hair almost stood on end. He gaped at Pacey.

'Gerald Ellis-Morgan!'

Pacey didn't wait to discuss it. 'Stay here. Miss Collins. Come on, Willie! '

As he turned the door knob, there was a knock on the panel and the door pushed open against his hand.

'They told me to come up, Mr Pacey – about the statement.'

Gerald Ellis-Morgan poked his head around the door and, as he saw Edna Collins standing in the room, a sickly smile spread over his face.

'Come in, Doctor, will you.'

Pacey's voice was unusually grim. His habitual air of easy bonhomie had evaporated and he closed the door and stood with his back to it as Gerald moved into the room.

The woman stood with her handbag pressed to her chest, watching the new arrival as if she expected him to whip a revolver from his pocket at any second. Rees stood near to the desk, bewilderment at Gerald's materialization plain on his face.

'Er … hello, again.' Gerald spoke sheepishly to the girl, who continued to stare at him as if petrified.

Pacey came to life, his voice cold and heavy.

'Dr Ellis-Morgan, I gather that you already know this young lady?'

Gerald, his manner suggesting embarrassment rather

than guilt, turned to the superintendent. 'Er … yes, we bumped into each other in the street just now.'

Pacey spoke slowly, as if to emphasize the importance of his words. 'But did you know her before then?'

Gerald looked from Pacey to Edna and back again.

'We had met – briefly. A very long time ago.'

The atmosphere in the room was tense. Rees and the barmaid looked like two springs, coiled ready to fly into action.

Pacey walked towards the doctor, who began to look more and more uncomfortable.

'And just where was it that you met, sir?'

Gerald's discomfiture began to change into annoyance. 'Really, Mr Pacey, I don't know what's going on here! I came to sign some statement for you. The fact that I happen to have met this lady a long time ago is no business of yours. I can't imagine why she's here, but it's no concern of mine.'

'I'm afraid it might well be, Doctor,' Pacey said tonelessly. 'I must ask you to answer my questions – and I assure you that it may be very much your business. Now, where and when did you first meet this lady?'

Gerald shrugged resignedly. 'OK. But I hope you'll keep my answers to yourself – I would take grave exception to my private life being broadcast. I met the lady – I'm afraid I can't remember her name – in Cardiff.'

'Where in Cardiff,' persisted Pacey inexorably.

'In a club, as it happens.' Gerald managed to inject a note of condescension into his voice.

'Would that be the "Porcupine Club"?' asked the detective.

'Yes, it was.'

'And when were you last there?'

Gerald looked genuinely puzzled. 'God, I don't know. Ages ago – must have been about nineteen fifty-four or five – when my brother was working in Cardiff.'

'And did you ever stay with your brother at his flat near the hospital?'

Gerald began to redden and look angry. 'What the hell is all this about? You seem to have been doing a great deal of snooping. Was this nonsense about a statement a trick to get me up here?'

Pacey sighed, relaxing his mood slightly. 'No, as it happens, it was not! Now, please, answer my question. Did you ever use your brother's flat? And, if so, when?'

Gerald dropped into a chair and slapped his hands on his thighs in exasperation.

'Why should I answer you? This is an intrusion into my private life. All right. So I did go to a rather offbeat club and I did borrow my brother's flat for the odd weekend. What's that got to do with you? What *is* all this?'

'You did stay there, then. Was your brother always there? And when was the last time you stayed there?'

Gerald got up again and walked up to Pacey until their noses were almost touching.

'Look, I do – not – know when I stayed there – it was bloody years ago – but I *do* know that I'm not going to answer any more damn fool questions!'

'Doctor, you're going to answer one more, whether you like it or not. Did you know a girl by the name of Julie Gordon?'

There was a silence as palpable as a concrete wall. Gerald's already indignantly pink face became even more flushed.

'I was wondering when you were going to get around to that!' he said, sarcasm and bitterness in his voice. 'I suppose it's almost inevitable, really – a respectable country practitioner isn't allowed to let his hair down occasionally without risking social suicide. I suppose this is something to do with a blackmail attempt. Is it this woman behind it?'

Pacey shook his head and motioned Rees to the door.

'Inspector, go out and see if you can catch Dr David Ellis-Morgan before he finishes his shopping. His car is in the yard. Ask him to come up here.'

Rees vanished and Pacey advanced to the middle of the room.

'I'm sorry, Doctor, but I should advise you not to say anything until your brother comes and you arrange to get a solicitor. You see, I'm afraid that I must formally charge you with the murder of Julie Ann Gordon, in November nineteen fifty-five and caution you that anything you say may be taken down and used in evidence.'

Chapter Eighteen

When Rees returned ten minutes later with the accused man's brother, Pacey took him into another room on the ground floor to break the news of Gerald's arrest.

Rees took Edna Collins away to get a proper statement drawn up, leaving Gerald Ellis-Morgan in the upper office in charge of a constable from the station.

Pacey gravely outlined to David the events leading up to the arrest of his brother.

'You see, sir, I thought all along – at least, ever since the Mavis Hewitt nonsense was dealt with – that there was a medical brain behind this affair.'

David listened in silence. His face was drained of every trace of colour, but his voice was firm and controlled.

'This is utter nonsense itself, Mr Pacey. But I suppose you must have some facts to lead you to such a foolhardy thing as to charge my brother with murder?'

'I have indeed, Doctor. This isn't a thing I'd undertake lightly. Your brother has already admitted knowing the dead girl's friend – the woman upstairs. He admits knowing the deceased girl – admits seeing her frequently during the last week of her life – admits staying in your flat that week, when you were absent for several nights. Now, sir, when the body is found not half a mile from your brother's home, in circumstances which make it almost certain that someone with medical knowledge is involved, what choice have I but to accuse him of the crime?'

David sat like a stone image, hands clasped so tightly that the knuckles showed white through the skin.

'It sounds as if my brother has done too much talking

already. I must get him a lawyer before he makes an even bigger fool of himself.'

Pacey was thankful that the older brother was taking this shocking experience in such a sensible way. By contrast, Gerald's reaction to being charged was a volatile mixture of scorn, anger and apprehension.

'I think it would be very wise to get a solicitor, as soon as possible. I'm afraid your brother is a rather hot-headed young man. He might let his temper provoke him into saying something which he might regret, unless you have someone to advise and restrain him.'

David rose from the chair abruptly. 'I'll see about it right away. But, tell me, you must have stronger evidence than the word of a barmaid and the mere admission of Gerry's that he had a passing acquaintance with the dead girl?'

Pacey saw no harm in revealing what would soon be common knowledge, in return for the civilized way in which the doctor was taking the disaster.

'We have indeed, sir. Our laboratory has identified human bloodstains on the floor of the bathroom in your old flat and also found blood in the outlet of the bath.'

He was diplomatic enough not to mention that the tests were done at a time when David himself was the suspect. Pacey also carefully refrained from mentioning the examination of the Ford estate car.

David took the news in silence. After a moment spent in staring unseeingly at the opposite wall, he turned to leave the room.

'Thank you for your consideration, Superintendent. I'll go and see about that solicitor now. I suppose Gerald will be kept here, won't he?'

Pacey nodded gravely. 'I'm afraid he will be kept in custody until remanded by a magistrate in the morning. Then he will have to wait for the preliminary hearing, which will be within a week or two. If the justices think there is a strong enough case, they will commit him to the next Assizes for trial.'

The two men looked directly at each other and their eyes clashed.

'I don't think matters will get as far as that, Mr Pacey. Remember Roland Hewitt? He was *another* red herring.' The doctor's voice held a biting challenge.

Pacey sighed. 'It doesn't give me any pleasure, if that's any comfort to you. Arresting your brother is a part of my job that I could quite easily do without. But I have to do what I think is right, sir.'

David walked to the door, and turned as he reached it. 'I think you mean that, Mr Pacey. Thank you. I'll go and fix up this solicitor now. I'll telephone you inside an hour to let you know what's been arranged. You won't question my brother before then, I hope?'

'No. I'll wait until I hear from you, Doctor.'

When David Ellis-Morgan had gone, Pacey went back to the office upstairs, where Gerald was nervously pacing the floor, smoking like a furnace. Pacey dismissed the stolid PC who stood on guard. As he left, Willie Rees came in with Edna Collins' statement.

'Would you like a cup of tea, Doctor?' asked Pacey, being unable himself to really believe that this normal-looking man had killed and mutilated a young woman.

'No, thanks. All I want is to see my solicitor and get this bloody nonsense cleared up. I've got no ill-will against you, Pacey, but this is too much this time! You sailed pretty near the wind with old Hewitt, but you've picked the wrong customer to antagonize in me!'

'Your brother has been in to see me. He's just gone out to organize a lawyer for you. I'm not going to ask you for a statement until he comes. And I advise you, off the record, not to say another thing until you get some legal advice.'

Gerald made no reply and strode to the window,

turning his back on them.

Rees showed Pacey the story as dictated by the blonde barmaid, and they spent a few minutes going through it.

'I'd better go and phone the chief constable,' said Pacey in a low voice. 'He'll go up in flames when he hears about this, but he's got to know sooner or later. You'd better come with me, so get that PC back in here. I don't like to see him standing so near that window. It's a long drop if he takes it into his head to jump.'

The two detectives went back to the office off the charge room and Pacey put a call through to Cardigan. The colonel was engaged and Pacey sat by the telephone ready to try later.

'What about the Press?' queried Willie. 'Poor Adams is going to be in a worse spot than ever – with his future brother-in-law on the spot, instead of his uncle!'

'Yes, I feel sorry for him – and for the sister and father, to say nothing of the other brother. He took it well, but you could see that the news just about tore him apart inside.'

The telephone rang and Pacey answered it, expecting the call to be Cardigan ringing back.

It was David Ellis-Morgan.

'Hello, Doctor. Have you managed to fix up your lawyer?'

David's voice came distantly over the line. 'No, Mr Pacey. That won't be necessary. In fact, it never was.'

Pacey felt the first hint of something wrong as a prickle at the back of his neck.

'I don't follow you, sir. What d'you mean by that?'

'If I were you, I'd just listen for a few minutes, Superintendent. Gerald knows nothing about this business – nothing at all.'

Pacey made frantic signalling gestures to attract Rees over from the other side of the room, while he carried on talking to the caller.

'I don't understand this at all, Doctor. Your brother

admitted knowing the dead girl, and being in her company during the last week that her movements were known.'

The detective understood perfectly well – the truth had burst upon him at the end of the first sentence that David Ellis-Morgan had uttered; but now he was stalling for time.

As Willie hurried across to the telephone, the distant voice began to speak again.

'He knew Julie Gordon all right. So did I – the little bitch!'

Pacey was scribbling on a piece of paper as he listened, with Rees leaning over him to see what he was writing.

'You'd better tell me the lot, Doctor. Where are you speaking from, by the way?'

Pacey tried to make his voice sound as casual and matter-of-fact as he could; but he was wasting his time.

'I'm afraid I won't be able to tell you that. You'll trace the call before long, I know. But, if you want to hear the truth, I'll have to have a few minutes grace.'

Pacey succeeded in scrawling a barely legible message for Rees. It read: "Trace call. Send any available patrol. Pick up David E-M. Urgent prevent escape or suicide."

Willie nodded and rushed off to the telephone switchboard in the charge room. Pacey contrived to listen to David while this was going on.

'Are you listening to me, Superintendent?' he asked sharply.

'Yes, I'm here. Go on.'

'You've already started to trace me, haven't you?' accused the doctor, correctly diagnosing the faltering attention of Pacey for a couple of moments. 'So I'll have to make it short and sweet. Don't interrupt me, please. This is the last chance you'll ever get of hearing the real truth, so make the most of it. Then you can let Gerald go – with some apologies, I hope.'

'I'm waiting, Doctor Ellis-Morgan.'

Pacey knew now that all he could do was to try to keep the other man talking long enough for Rees to contact a patrol car and pick David up. The man had only been gone from the police station a matter of twenty minutes, so couldn't be very far away.

'Gerry had picked up this girl and brought her back to the flat I had in Cardiff on several occasions when I was out on duty. This was earlier in the week – that last awful week.'

For the first time, the iron control of David's voice weakened momentarily.

'Why was your brother in Cardiff, anyway?' Pacey was both seeking information and trying to prolong the talking.

'He used to come up to stay with me a few times a year – long weekends and an occasional week. He was fond of a bit of city life after his student days in London, and he found Tremabon a bit of a dead hole for the first few years. He used to sleep in the flat. I usually found myself a bed in the hospital when I was on emergency call. I found out later that he had picked up this Julie in a club and brought her back there on several nights until the early hours ... but I didn't know it at the time. On the Friday morning, he had a phone message calling him back to Tremabon. Dad had caught the 'flu and Gerry had to go back a couple of days early to run the practice.'

Pacey looked at his watch – it was four minutes since the telephone had rung. Why the devil didn't Willie come back and tell him what was happening?

'You're still there, Pacey?' David's voice sounded anxious.

'Yes, don't worry. I still don't know what all this is about. I hope you're not wasting the time of both of us by inventing some far-fetched defence for your brother, sir.'

'No defence needed, Mr Pacey. I had no intention of going for a lawyer when I left you just now. I could have told you all this sitting in your office. But, then, you would have stopped me from doing what I have to do very soon. This was the only way to get clear of you. Yes, I killed Julie Gordon, Mr Pacey. On the Friday night, after Gerry had gone, she came to the flat. He had arranged to meet her somewhere, but failed to get a message through to her. So she turned up to look for him. I didn't know who, or what, she was then. Gerry didn't talk much about affairs of that sort – he was a bit ashamed of his easy pick-ups. Anyway, to cut a long story short – it will have to be, Mr Pacey, now that you've got the police force out looking for me – to get right to the point, I took over where my brother left off. She came into my flat to explain. We had a drink together. One thing led to another and she didn't leave that night. In fact, she didn't leave at all – alive.'

Pacey was genuinely gripped now, without thought of his patrol cars closing in.

'What happened?' he asked tensely.

'We made quite a party of it that night. It was all the more exciting to me, as I haven't got Gerry's easy way with women. She was very attractive and made up for the scores of lonely, miserable nights I'd spent in that flat alone. We got a little drunk, then we went to bed. It was after that the trouble began. Whether it was conscience or fear, I don't know, but I sobered up quickly and felt revolted at myself. I tried to get her to go, but she began to turn nasty. She was still a bit drunk – bitchy and vicious. The more I tried to get rid of her, the worse she got. Then she began saying things – how would our father like it if he knew both his sons were sleeping with club hostesses – that it might cost us both a packet for her to keep her mouth shut. Looking back on it, I'm sure she wasn't really serious, but just drunk and showing off. Anyway, at the time, it made me see red, mainly because it was true – two respectable medical men carrying on like that – and my part was worse than Gerry's, by far; I almost felt that I was cuckolding my own brother.'

Pacey waited, both for the other to go on and for Rees to come back.

'One thing led to another and she started shouting and sneering and shrieking. God it was awful! I shook her and slapped her and she yelled all the more, taunting me with what I'd done – and other things!'

Pacey guessed what the 'other things' were.

'And then?' he prompted, cursing Rees under his breath.

'Before I knew what was happening, I had her by the throat, trying to shut her up. It was about one in the morning and the flat is right next to the hospital. I was afraid someone would hear her. The next thing, she was limp in my hands. I did everything I could – artificial respiration, heart massage – but she was dead. She just slumped down. It couldn't have been strangulation, just shock from pressure on her neck.'

He paused, even the impersonal wires of a telephone carrying the seven-year-old emotions in his words clearly to Pacey.

'Believe me – not that it matters now – I had no intention of killing her. I was just scared and angry at the bloody things she was saying.'

At last Willie Rees hurried back into the room. Pacey put a finger to his lips to keep him silent; so the inspector, in his turn, scribbled a message:

"Phoning from public box at Tremabon. Nearest patrol at serious accident, Llanmaes, ten miles away."

Pacey rolled his eyes up at Rees in frustration. At times like these, he envied the big city forces that always had a car within three minutes of anywhere – not like the rural areas where it was difficult even to keep cars within range of the radio transmitters.

He forced himself back to listen to the confessions of the doctor.

'... in the bathroom, while I thought out some plan. I sat there all night. I must have had some sort of mad frenzy just after I did it, as I found myself with a surgical saw from the plaster clinic downstairs, standing by the bath with blood everywhere and her arm almost off. That pulled me together more than anything else could have. I sat down and thought all night, then locked myself in the bathroom while the cleaner came in the morning – so that she wouldn't see anything. Then, gradually, the plan about Mavis Hewitt came to me.'

'How did you know about that?'

'I heard it years before from Ceri Lloyd and someone else in the village – I used to go to the pub quite a bit when I was a student, home on vacation. The idea came to me to hide the body in a mine – I knew plenty from the days when Gerry and I used to play on the cliffs as boys. I knew Roland was the suspect, even though there was no proof that she was dead. And Roland had gone abroad years before, and everyone in the village seemed sure that he had died long ago. So I decided to insure myself against the body being found by faking it up as Mavis Hewitt.'

Pacey looked at the hands of his watch creeping round. Even if the nearest car could leave the scene of a serious accident straight away, it would take ten or twelve minutes at least to reach David Ellis-Morgan, going at seventy miles an hour – which was an almost impossible speed on the country roads.

'What happened – how did you manage to fool us so well?'

'I remembered from Ceri's yarn that Mavis was in her twenties when she vanished. I also knew that she was a redhead; Ceri was very clear about that. I stripped her clothes off, cut off all the dark hair and washed it down the lavatory.

'Then I went out to a theatrical costumier and got a set of clothes from the nineteen twenties – insisted on having authentic stuff. I said it was for an amateur production of one of Somerset Maugham's plays. I hunted around for some pawnbrokers in the dock area and got some old-fashioned jewellery and a wedding ring with as near correct hallmark date as I could.'

'How did you get rid of the bloodstained clothes?'

Pacey made no attempt to challenge the truth of all these revelations – there could be no doubt as to that. His only concern was to keep David talking for another ten or fifteen minutes.

'The clothes? That was easy. I wrapped them up, took them over to the hospital mortuary and dumped them on the floor. There are always heaps of old clothes, often bloody, lying around, from accident cases. Every now and then, the attendants collect them up and take them to the incinerator. Another odd heap would go unnoticed.'

'And the teeth – how did you get around that?'

'Yes, that was difficult – she had three fillings, so I took them out together with another two spares. I was physically sick doing that, even though I earned part of my living in dissecting bodies. Still, it had to be done, not only for my own sake, but also to cover up for Gerry and to save my father and Mary from the ruin of the practice and their home.'

'Well, that's going to happen now, isn't it?' grated Pacey.

'We've had seven years, better than nothing. I'm sorry though.'

The voice sounded far off and Pacey began to think that, at last, the doctor's mind was beginning to crack. He looked at the hands of his watch again, crawling with a microscopic motion around the dial. He picked up his pencil and scrawled "PC Griffith?" on his pad.

He looked up at Willie, who nodded, shook his head and shrugged his shoulders, all in rapid succession. Pacey interpreted this as meaning that Rees had already thought of it, but could not get through to the Tremabon constable on the telephone for some reason.

David was talking again, and Pacey turned his attention back to him.

'I also bought a switch of real auburn hair in the theatrical shop. I went back to the flat, waited until dark and loaded the body, wrapped in a hospital sheet, into the back of my Ford.'

'We tested that for stains yesterday – there were none. How did you manage that?' asked Pacey.

'So you did suspect me? Why?'

Pacey added a moment or two to his valuable delaying tactics by explaining this, then asked about the blood again.

'There was almost no bleeding by the time I moved her. I covered the wound in the arm with an adhesive surgical dressing, then – wrapped an old plastic mackintosh around it under the sheet. I brought them both back and dumped them in the mortuary, like the other stuff.'

David Ellis-Morgan sounded almost too anxious to talk, thought Pacey. The words were tumbling out of his mouth as he stood alone in the red telephone box in Tremabon. He knew as well as Pacey that the time he had left before the patrol car reached him could be measured in minutes. He talked in a rush now, the mental purging flowing like a breached dam – a dam that had held firm against communication with even a single person for the last seven years.

'I drove back to Tremabon that night, took the car past Bryn Glas Farm and up the track to the cliff. I put the lights out for the last bit across the moor and got within a few hundred yards of the cave before the going got too bad for the car. Then I carried the bundle to the cave – and left it on the ground, well inside. I had to chance it being found before the next morning, when I went back there. I drove the car back to the road and then deliberately ran into a gatepost to buckle the front wing.'

Pacey was puzzled at this, curiosity getting the better of his constant study of his watch.

'I was shaken and it was late. I had to have some excuse for turning up at home after midnight, shaking like a leaf. I said I'd had a slight accident – that covered up well enough.'

'Did you tell Gerald anything about all this?'

'No! He knows nothing – nothing at all.' The voice cracked sharply and emphatically over the wire. 'He didn't come up to Cardiff to stay again – I made excuses and, as soon as I could, I left the job and came back home.'

Pacey began stalling. 'You said that you left the body on the floor of the cave. How did it get up on the ledge?'

'I went for a walk from the house next day. There was nothing unusual in that; I often did when I was home for a weekend. I went straight up to the mine, put the body up on the ledge – I knew it was there from explorations as a kid. Then I bricked it in with stones and went home. If it wasn't for that fall of roof, it would be there still.'

It was nine minutes since Rees had notified the patrol car. Pacey searched for something intelligent to say to keep Ellis-Morgan talking.

'Look, you'd better talk to your brother – hang on, I'll get him from the other room.' He motioned to Rees to do what he had said and the inspector sprinted away.

'There may not be time for that, Mr Pacey. And I don't think I want to talk to him – what could I say?'

'You could say you're sorry for rushing off and leaving him here to carry the can for you, for a. start,' Pacey said, almost roughly. 'And then you could tell him that you're coming back here right away to get things sorted out. You silly ass, if you'd have gone to the police at the time, you would have walked away with a plea of manslaughter, with a defence of provocation like that. And you've a very good chance of doing it yet, if you come back here and act

212

sensibly.'

There was a sad, humourless laugh from the other end, a laugh with more than a hint of hysteria in it.

'Keeping me talking, Mr Pacey? Unfortunately, I'm in a phone box at the bottom of the lane leading up to Bryn Glas and the cliff, with a view of almost a mile of the main road in both directions. Your patrol car hasn't appeared, not yet. When I hang up, you can assume that it has!'

'What are you going to do, man? Don't be a damn fool! Come on in. Wait for the car and come back with the officers. I tell you, you'll get away with manslaughter in a case like this.'

'And what do I do when I come out of prison in five years' time, become a bricklayer? No thank you, Superintendent.'

'You can't get away. Don't be idiotic.'

Pacey knew how Ellis-Morgan was going to get away, but he was unable to admit it, either to himself or to the doctor.

'Sorry, I know what I'm doing. I've been on the verge of it more than once, in the first year or two – and then I thought I might have gotten away with it.'

Twelve minutes. The door opened and Rees hurriedly shepherded a worried and mystified Gerald into the room.

'Here, come and talk to your brother, for God's sake! Make him see sense – he's threatening to kill himself. He was the one responsible for the death of the woman in the cave – Julie Gordon.'

Gerald almost fell down with shock. He groped for the telephone which Pacey held out for him and sank onto the chair as the detective made way for him.

He looked up at Pacey for a moment, his face almost green, then put the receiver to his ear.

'Dave – Dave, this is Gerry. Dave, Dave! Hello, David!'

He rattled the button and almost shouted David*s name

a few times, then looked fearfully up at the superintendent. 'He's hung up – Dave's hung up!' he whispered.

Chapter Nineteen

A double inquest was held in the church hall at Tremabon on the following Monday.

The small building was packed with newspaper reporters and morbid spectators from far and wide. If the case had made very few headlines while it was being investigated, it was certainly making up for lost time now that it was all over ...

The first case was that of Julie Gordon. The main evidence came from Pacey, who had been the only witness to the oral confession of Doctor David Ellis-Morgan. Professor Powell, a senior scientific officer from the Swansea laboratory and Edna Collins gave other confirmatory facts and the coroner's very imperative directions to his jury ensured that a verdict of murder by David Ellis-Morgan was brought in with a minimum of the dilly-dallying so beloved of coroner's juries ...

The disposal of the woman was followed by the inquiry into the death of the doctor himself.

Two county mobile policemen described how, in answer to an urgent radio call from Detective-Superintendent Pacey, they went at high speed from Llanmaes to Tremabon, with orders to take into custody the occupant of a telephone box at the junction of the main road with the lane leading up to Bryn Glas farm and the open moorland beyond.

As Pacey, sitting in the front of the court, heard the dry official description from the patrol sergeant, his mind translated it into the real scene, so abruptly cut off from his room in Aberystwyth by the deadening of a telephone line.

As the black police car appeared almost a mile away, racing along at something over seventy miles an hour, David must have slammed the telephone down and run out to his waiting car. The police saw nothing of the Austin-Healey until it broke from the cover of the hedges of the lane and went bumping out onto the moor. They lost precious seconds by stopping at the telephone box. It was only then, with their own motor cut, that they heard the roaring acceleration of the doctor's powerful engine going up the lane. Until then, they had no idea that he was still in the vicinity. Racing after him in their heavier and slower saloon, they were a good quarter of a mile behind when they, too, broke from the hedges of the lane onto the open rough ground.

The two cars, bouncing and jerking, headed straight up the long slope that formed the back of the cliffs. Though the two mobile officers did not know it at the time, the Austin-Healey was retracing the route the doctor had taken seven years before in his Ford estate car. But on that occasion, he had stopped short of the head of the little valley down from the crest of the cliff past the old lead mine. This time, the red sports car entered the neck of the gully at thirty miles an hour and plunged, rocking and swaying, down the seaward side. By the time it reached the place where the grass ended and the scree slopes began, it was doing almost sixty. The gravelly scree ended in a sheer two hundred-foot wall and the car shot out in a long parabola into the air above the breakers below. Pacey saw in his mind's eye, the car slowly turning over and over as it fell, far out beyond the rocks at the foot of the cliff.

The police car, unfamiliar with the sudden change from moorland to cliff, rocked and skidded dangerously to a stop just in time to avoid following the Austin-Healey down the valley. The policemen ran down the track of crushed ferns and muddy wheel tracks to the edge of the precipice.

Far below, they could see nothing at first. Even the great splash of a few moments before had been swallowed by the restless waves. But, soon, a rainbow patch of motor oil appeared and two foam rubber seat cushions floated free from the drowned car.

The body, firmly held by a safety belt, was recovered at low tide, twisted and broken like the car itself.

Little other evidence was needed and the jury again speedily returned their verdict, one of 'suicide while the balance of his mind was disturbed,' the last part having more of a traditional than a logical significance. After the formalities were over, and the reporters had trooped off to their telephones and typewriters, the chief constable, Pacey and the professor went into the little side room used by the coroner for a last few words.

'A sensible jury, for once – didn't try to make a meal out of it,' observed the coroner.

'I suppose the papers are bound to splash it for a day or two – they always do when it's a doctor or a clergyman involved,' said Colonel Barton.

'There's no manhunt involved, or prospect of a trial, now,' added Pacey. 'So the Press will soon lose interest.'

'The sooner the better, for the sake of the family,' commented Barton. 'The young idiot could have saved a lot of distress if he'd acted sensibly seven years ago'

Pacey grimaced. 'All this from an hour's guilty pleasure with some damn barmaid. But, even if he had owned up then, there'd have been a devil of a scandal!'

The coroner nodded. 'I can still hardly believe it – I've known old John Ellis-Morgan for years. As you say, this would have been a terrible splash, even at the time of the death. I don't know that they're not better off as it is - at least it's all over in one go. The other way it would have been "Local doctor sent for trial on passion killing" –

headlines a foot high. It would have ruined old John and Gerald, as far as their practice went.'

'Well, you can hardly say it's done them much good as it is,' the colonel said stubbornly. 'What will they do now, I wonder?'

The coroner answered this one. 'I understand that the old man is going to give up right away – he's only a year off retiring, anyway. Gerald says he is going to sell up the house as soon as possible and either go off to England with his father or even abroad altogether. They've got nothing to keep them here now, as Mary is putting her wedding forward and will be off to Cardiff to live.'

Pacey sighed. 'I suppose the whole affair will grow and mature into another Cardiganshire legend, like the sunken land under the bay there – Ceri Lloyd and his crew will have enough scandal to chew over in the bar for the rest of their miserable lives.' The superintendent sounded bitter.

There was a thoughtful silence for a moment, then the chief constable spoke almost chirpily. 'Well, Pacey, if we've gained nothing else from this case, we've learned not to jump to conclusions and look for facts to fit to them, eh?'

Pacey put a hand to his forehead to hide a scowl.

'Yes, sir,' he muttered. 'We have, haven't we!'

Powell grinned at the detective. 'You mean a string of beads and a couple of old pennies don't make a seven-year-old corpse become thirty-three, eh?'

Pacey grunted, quite unamused.

'But surely,' asked the coroner, 'if that body had been found, say a year after death, you could have said that it couldn't possibly be twenty or more years old – so he took a dickens of a risk, didn't he?'

'It was Hobson's choice, I suppose,' answered the professor. 'He was stuck with a body. He knew, probably from talking to her, that she had no immediate family to miss her, so this Mavis Hewitt lark was a second line of defence. He hoped that no one would find the body, in his lifetime, but if they did, after a few years, they would be foxed into thinking it was, firstly, too old to be connected with him. And, secondly, was Mavis Hewitt. And he almost succeeded, too, we must give him credit for that, if "credit" is the only word we can use.'

Pacey added his own postscript. 'If that X-ray and bit of Terylene thread hadn't turned up, we might have clapped old Hewitt into jail for the rest of his natural.'

He paused.

'All the same, I'd give a lot to know what really *did* happen to Mavis Hewitt.'

THE END

The Sixties Mysteries
by
Bernard Knight

The Lately Deceased
The Thread of Evidence
Mistress Murder
Russian Roulette
Policeman's Progress
Tiger at Bay
The Expert

For more information about **Bernard Knight**

and other **Accent Press** titles

please visit

www.accentpress.co.uk

Bruce County Public Library
1243 Mackenzie Rd.
Port Elgin ON N0H 2C6

CPSIA information can be obtained
at www.ICGtesting.com
Printed in the USA
LVOW12s2016010916

502845LV00001B/23/P